THE THOUSAND-MILE JOURNEY

The story of a brave Labrador, an incredible
journey and a little girl's faith

A Novel
by
Ed Dunlop

Printed and Bound in the United States of America

CONTENTS

Chapter 1

VACATION

Alice Patterson glanced out across the surging breakers, worry clouding her sparkling blue eyes. Two small heads bobbed in the water close to two brightly colored inflatable rafts. A shriek of delight floated across the beach as a wave lifted the youngsters high, then dropped them abruptly. A huge black Labrador retriever romped in the breakers, barking and snapping at the foaming waves.

The woman glanced back at the inert form of her husband, then gave voice to her fears. "Don't you think the kids are getting out a little too far?"

"They'll be okay," the man reassured her. "David swims like a fish, and Christina's gonna be a little mermaid before we know it. Besides, Prince is with them! What can happen?"

Still worried, the mother watched the trio in the water for another moment, then went back to the mystery novel she was reading.

Moments later, the big dog trotted across the deserted beach, tired of his romp in the surf. He approached the couple on the beach blanket with a happy grin on his canine face, then proceeded to shake vigorously, showering the two startled vacationers with cold seawater.

"Prince!" the woman screamed. "You shaggy dog! Get away! You've soaked everything!"

The man rolled over on his back, put on his glasses, then, with an effort, sat up. Thirteen years earlier, in the heart of Beirut, Lebanon, a sniper's bullet had caught him in the back. He had returned from his tour of duty with his legs partially paralyzed.

Six months after his return from Beirut, he had married his childhood sweetheart, the beautiful Alice O'Dell, and landed the teaching position at Bakersfield.

He reached for the dog, who plopped down on the blanket beside him. "Go easy, Mrs. Patterson," the man said, smiling. "Prince didn't mean any harm, did you, old boy?" The huge tail thumped on the blanket, leaving a wet imprint on the fabric. "He's just inviting you to share the water with him!"

Mrs. Patterson's face darkened. "Kenneth, that's not funny! You know I'm terrified of the water. I really wish you wouldn't let the kids go out quite so far!" The look she gave the big, dripping dog made it clear that she was not especially fond of the animal. Prince was a favorite with the other three members of the Patterson family, but Mrs. Patterson barely tolerated him.

Mr. Patterson adjusted his glasses and glanced toward the shiny new Ford pickup camper parked at the upper end of the beach. The vehicle represented years of scrimping and saving, and he felt considerable pride in the accomplishment of acquiring it. The truck was the first new vehicle the Pattersons had ever owned and, on his salary as professor of computer sciences at Bakersfield Community College, would probably be the last. He sighed, trying not to remember that tomorrow would be the last day of vacation.

He shifted his attention to the boy and girl playing in the water. Ten-year-old David, floating on a bright blue air mattress, was tall and thin like his father with the same dark hair and eyes. Six-year-old Christina, a small, blonde replica of her mother, complete with fair skin, blue eyes and freckles, was bobbing nearby on a yellow raft.

As Mr. Patterson watched, David lay down on his raft and began to paddle furiously. An incoming breaker caught the trailing edge of the raft and began to propel the little craft toward the beach. The boy let out a whoop as he and the raft picked up speed.

The man glanced out toward his daughter, then sucked in his breath sharply. "Christina's in trouble!" He reached for his crutches.

As he struggled awkwardly to his feet, his wife exploded into action. Sandled feet flying, she dashed toward the water, her lacy, pink dress trailing merrily in the breeze behind her. "David!" she screamed. "Help Christina!"

The little girl had fallen from her raft into the water, clutched at the raft, then lost her grip. Just then, a breaker hit her from behind, jerking the rubber raft beyond her reach. She disappeared beneath the water, then reappeared, choking and gasping. The current spun her around, then began to tow her toward deeper water.

Mr. Patterson hobbled awkwardly across the beach. The soft sand hindered his progress with the crutches.

"Help her, Kenneth!" Mrs. Patterson screamed as her husband reached her side. "She's drowning!"

Mr. Patterson looked at his wife helplessly. Her overwhelming terror of water kept her from even setting foot in the waves, and he knew that he was just as helpless. His crippled legs were useless in the water. "Dear Lord," he prayed aloud, "save my little girl! We can't do anything, and there's not another soul in sight!" His voice broke as he was overcome by his emotions.

Realizing that an emergency was at hand, young David leaped back into the waves, throwing his body on top of his raft and paddling furiously. But the force of the breakers was against him. The same ocean current compelling his little sister out to disaster was determined to toss him back out on the beach like a battered piece of driftwood. He struggled bravely but seemed to be getting nowhere.

Little Christina was terrified. Choking and coughing, she screamed for help, then was pushed brutally beneath the surface by a powerful wave.

Chapter 2

THE RESCUE

Christina's screams pierced the tranquility of the afternoon as the treacherous undertow carried her farther from the beach. Then her voice was silenced as a foaming breaker closed over her head with the speed and force of an express train. For several heart-stopping seconds, her struggling form disappeared from view.

Her brother had finally crossed through the first line of breakers but was advancing very slowly against the currents. He would never make it out to her in time, but he fought gamely, his tired, thin arms still flailing the water.

Mr. and Mrs. Patterson watched in horrified silence, then suddenly Mr. Patterson swung his crutches forward and hobbled into the surf. He had a determined glint in his eye, as if he were a soldier going into battle. His wife gasped, then leaped into the shallow water and clutched at his arm.

"Kenneth," she screamed, "what are you doing? There's nothing you can do! You'll never make it!"

With a sudden lunge, the tall man pulled free of her grasp. "I've got to go!" he insisted. "Christina..." A sudden sob cut off his words.

At that instant a powerful black form leaped over an advancing wave and landed in the water with a huge splash. Forgotten by the rest of the family, the mighty Labrador had heard his little mistress' screams and was going to her rescue. Prince had entered the battle.

Mr. Patterson retreated from the surf and stood beside his wife, tears streaming down his cheeks, watching the brave dog fight his way through the pounding breakers. Both parents suddenly realized that Christina's only hope was Prince. If the dog could not reach her in time, she was lost. Suddenly finding their voices, they began to scream encouragement to the dog.

"Hang on, Honey!" Mrs. Patterson called to her daughter. "Prince is coming!" But her words were lost in the roar of the ocean.

The huge dog struggled fiercely toward the girl, his huge paws flailing the water in powerful strokes. Inch by inch, he was slowly closing the gap. But he was still some forty yards away, and the little girl was out of time. He would reach her, but it would be too late.

Miraculously, the powerful currents suddenly threw the bobbing yellow raft within reach of the terrified girl, and her thrashing arms closed tightly around it. Her head finally clear of the water, she choked and coughed, then began to suck in huge lungfuls of the precious air. It was as though the whimsical sea, tired of playing its cruel game, had mercifully chosen to return the inflatable to its desperate little owner.

New hope sprang up in the hearts of the two frantic parents watching helplessly from the shore. The raft would buy Christina at least a moment or two of precious time. Perhaps Prince would reach her in time after all. They both prayed fervently.

Moments later, with a bark of joy, the big dog swam to the little girl's side. Immediately she released her hold on the yellow raft and grabbed the Labrador's collar with both chubby hands. "Swim, Prince!" she cried. "Swim!"

Tears of joy and relief coursed down the cheeks of both parents as Christina emerged from the surf, still clutching the leather collar of the valiant Prince. Mr. Patterson pried her fingers from the collar, hugged her fiercely, then laid her in the warm sand, still gasping and shaking. "Thank You, dear Lord," he whispered.

Mrs. Patterson glanced toward the ocean, then screamed in alarm. "David's still out there!" Her face paled as she pointed.

Mr. Patterson struggled to his feet, grimacing as he took in the situation at a glance. Paddling to his sister's aid, David had finally made it through the violence of the breakers. The blue raft now bobbed far out on the water, just beyond the last line of breakers. The current was taking him farther out every second.

Chapter 3
LOW TIDE

"Prince!" Mr. Patterson shouted. "Get David!" He pointed to the bobbing figure in the distance. "Go, boy!"

The panting dog needed no second command. He plunged back into the surf to attempt another rescue.

Several minutes later David, still floating on the blue raft, had a firm grip on Prince's collar and was being towed to shore. A cheer met them as a speeding wave deposited boy, dog and raft safely on the beach.

* * *

Supper that evening was a joyous occasion. The flames of the campfire popped and crackled as fat from the roasting hot dogs dripped into the fire. David and Christina, dressed in clean, dry clothes, seemed unharmed by their terrifying ordeal. They chattered happily as they crouched beside the fire, rotating the fat dogs on greasewood sticks.

"You dear, dear dog!" Mrs. Patterson had crooned to Prince on the beach that afternoon, her tears falling into his fur. "I'm sorry for the things I've said about you! Can you ever forgive me?" Prince had nobly licked her hand, and she insisted Prince have steak. He lay close to the children, happily gulping a one-pound T-bone.

Mr. Patterson smiled happily as he watched the dog devouring the steak. Prince was now a full-fledged member of the family, accepted and appreciated even by Mrs. Patterson.

His mind went back to the cold, rainy April afternoon just over a year before, when he had brought the squirming little Labrador puppy into the house. He held his breath in anticipation of the reception the animal would receive at the hands of his wife. The kids had responded with shrieks of joy when the struggling animal had emerged from the huge pocket of his raincoat, but his wife had responded as expected—she did not want the Labrador. Finally she gave in. The dog would stay—but never, under any circumstances, would he be allowed in the house.

The campfire was dying, and the coals were flashing orange and yellow in their death struggles when Mrs. Patterson scooted closer to her husband's seat on a log. "I never thought I'd ever say this," she whispered, "but thanks for bringing that puppy home in the rain last year." Mr. Patterson nodded happily.

Early the next morning Mr. Patterson reached up into the bunk over the cab of the truck and gently shook David and Christina awake.

"Get up quietly," he whispered. "This is our last day at the beach, and we want to make the most of it! Get dressed quietly and come outside. I want to show you something really special."

He quietly opened the camper door, and Mrs. Patterson rolled over in bed. "Kenneth, what's wrong?"

"Nothing," he whispered. "Go back to sleep. I'm just taking the kids down to the beach. It's low tide right now."

"I'll have breakfast ready when you get back," she promised.

He smiled and nodded. "Give us a good hour then." He quietly eased his crutches out the door and gently closed it behind him, then sat down on a log to wait for the kids. David and his sister popped out the door of the camper moments later, and the three of them strolled across the sand toward the water. Prince joined them, barking and racing in tight circles, excited at the prospect of an early outing.

"Daddy, it's cold!" Christina complained.

Dad laughed and tossed them each a sweater. "Here," he said. "Dad always comes prepared!"

The kids wriggled into the sweaters, and Christina suddenly stopped in amazement. She stared at the ocean. "Daddy, where did all the water go?"

The tall professor laughed. "It's low tide right now, Sweetheart. In the next hour or two, the water will come back up to where it usually is when we see it. But right now we have an excellent opportunity to catch some sea life."

The water had receded some hundred yards from the beach, and a jumble of round, dark rocks was now visible at the water's edge. Dad pointed. "Let's go out on the rocks," he suggested. "I think we'll find some interesting sea creatures."

He suddenly turned to David. "I forgot the buckets!" he told the boy. "Run back to camp and get them, will you? There's three of them under the front end of the camper. But try not to wake Mom."

David joined them out on the rocks a few moments later. Dad was helping Christina from rock to rock, crossing the shallow tide pools. Prince was tearing back and forth through the water, stopping occasionally to sniff at something here or bark at something there. The air was cool but smelled fresh and clean. The sun was just peeking over the rolling hills to the east, and the golden rays made the incoming breakers sparkle and glisten like the contents of a gigantic treasure chest.

"Look, Daddy, there's a starfish!" Christina squealed. Mr. Patterson transferred one crutch to the other hand, then reached over and picked it up. "Will it bite you?" the little girl worried. Her father assured her that it wouldn't.

"Can we take it home, Dad?" David asked.

"Sure," Mr. Patterson answered. "We'll get some baking soda from Mom when we get back, and I'll show you how to dry them out."

"Is it alive, Daddy?" Christina asked, her mouth drawn into a tight little circle. When her father nodded, she burst into tears. "I don't want David to kill it!" she wailed.

David shrugged, then set the bright orange creature back into the shallow water. "We won't hurt it then, okay?" he said gently, but his father could see the disappointment on his face.

Two large, clumsy-looking gray birds came skimming over the water just then, flying just ten or fifteen feet above the breakers. The professor pointed them out to the kids. "What are they, Dad?" David asked. "They look like air force bombers."

Dad chuckled. "They're pelicans," he replied. "Those guys are some of the best fishermen in the world. Hey! Watch!"

One of the birds emerged from the water with a wriggling fish in his bill and then dropped it. The kids laughed. "See that big pouch under his chin?" Dad said. "He'll store the fish in that pouch."

The three of them watched as the birds flew down the coast, occasionally diving into the surf for another addition to their meal.

Dad suddenly bent over and picked up a deep-crimson starfish. He examined it, then handed it to David. "This one's dead," he explained. "You can take it home, and even Christina won't complain."

"Daddy, can you find me one?" the little girl asked. Within minutes, David had found her a dead one.

David took off his socks and shoes, placed them on top of a large rock jutting from the water, then rolled up the cuffs of his jeans and began to wade. Christina suddenly decided to do the same. She filled her bucket with water. "I'm gonna catch a fish!" she declared.

"Let me show you how to do it then," Dad suggested.

"Lay your bucket on its side in the water beside that big flat rock. I'll raise the rock slowly, and if anything is hiding under the rock, it will try to find a new hiding place. Maybe it will go into your bucket."

The little girl grinned in anticipation. While David watched skeptically, Christina placed the bucket in the water as her father had directed. "Ready?" he asked. "Here goes! If anything goes into your bucket, jerk it up out of the water!"

Mr. Patterson inserted the tip of a crutch under the edge of the rock and, using another rock as a prop, slowly raised it. Suddenly a dark shape shot out from under the rock and zoomed into the bucket! "Pull it up!" her father cried. "Pull it up!"

"We caught one! We caught one!" the girl squealed in excitement. She bent her blonde head over the bucket, peering into the water. "Ooh!" she exclaimed. "What is it?"

Her brother took the bucket from her. "Let me see," he requested. Suddenly an expression of amazement passed across his features. "Dad!" he shouted. "We caught an octopus! We caught an octopus!"

He handed the bucket to his father, who studied the strange-looking creature in the pail. The animal was small, six or eight inches across. A round, bulbous head in the center was surrounded by eight writhing tentacles, the undersides of which were covered with rows and rows of tiny round suction cups. "You're right, Son," the man said in surprise, "it is an octopus!"

He turned to Christina, who was standing in the water with her mouth open. "You caught an octopus, Sweetheart!"

The girl clapped her hands in delight. "Oh, goody!" she exclaimed. "Let's catch another one!"

Dad laughed and handed her the bucket. "Well, we can try," he agreed.

Prince came bounding up just then and sprayed them all as he vigorously shook the salt water from his fur. Christina insisted on showing him the octopus, and he barked and barked.

They proceeded from rock to rock, hoping to catch another of the strange-looking sea animals. David and Christina would each place a bucket beside a likely-looking rock, then Mr. Patterson would raise it with a crutch. By the time the tide was beginning to cover the rocks half an hour later, they had made two more catches. David caught an octopus that was nearly twelve inches across, and Christina caught one that was slightly smaller than her first.

Finally Dad looked at his watch and suggested that it was time for breakfast.

Christina turned the one empty bucket upside down and sat on it to put on her socks and shoes. Prince came over and licked her face, and she wrapped her little arms around his massive neck in a passionate hug. "I love you, Prince!" she crooned to the big dog. "I'm glad you're part of our family!" He licked her face again. It was obvious that there was a very special bond between the two.

Chapter 4

CLOSE CALL

Back at camp, Christina excitedly showed her catch to her mother, who wrinkled her nose in disgust and asked, "What are they?"

"Octopuses!" the little girl happily informed her mother. "I caught them!"

"The plural form of *octopus* is *octopi*," her father corrected. "One *octopus*, two *octopi*."

"But we have three octopuses!" the little blonde declared, and everyone laughed. As David placed the creatures in their buckets under the camper, his sister showed her mother the starfish. "Daddy says we need baking soda," she explained.

The family ate breakfast at the little picnic table behind the camper. Mr. Patterson was amused to notice that his wife kept slipping bits of food to Prince, who was stationed under the table. "You never did that before," he observed dryly.

Mrs. Patterson laughed, slightly embarrassed. "Prince and I are gonna become good friends, aren't we, boy?"

"You wouldn't have done that a year ago!" Dad chuckled.

"Well," she defended herself, "Prince and I just got off to a bad start! But we're gonna become good friends, aren't we, Prince?"

The last day of vacation passed quickly—too quickly. The family spent most of the morning adding to their growing collection of seashells and sand dollars, and the kids went for one last cautious swim after lunch. Mrs. Patterson insisted that they stay close to shore and called them back when the water was just past their knees. She sat in her chaise lounge just a yard or two from the water's edge and never took her eyes from them. Prince romped with them in the surf.

That evening as the family sat down to a supper of corn dogs and applesauce, Dad turned to David and Christina. "We're gonna head home tonight," he told them. "It's about a five-hour drive, so we'll get home after dark."

"Couldn't we stay here just one more night?" David pleaded.

Dad shook his head. "I've got some business to attend to tomorrow, then we have church on Sunday. Remember, I have to be back on campus first thing Monday morning." He glanced over at Mom for support, and she nodded in agreement.

The gear was quickly packed after supper, and

Christina returned the three octopi to the ocean. Then, with a final longing look at the beach, the family climbed into the camper for the trip home. Prince was placed in the back of the camper by himself, while David and Christina squeezed in between their parents in the cab of the truck.

"I wish Prince could ride up here with us," the little girl said wistfully, as the camper pulled onto the highway. "He'll get lonely back there by his lonesome."

Mom laughed. "It's a bit crowded up here right now, even without Prince," she pointed out. "Where would we put him?"

"He could sit in your lap," Christina suggested, and the others laughed at the idea of Mom holding the ninety-pound dog in her lap during the five-hour trip.

Fifteen minutes later, Dad pulled off the highway. "Might as well get gas right now," he told the others. "Then if you want to sleep as we drive, I won't wake you up stopping for gas."

As Dad was pumping the gas, David and Christina opened the camper door to let Prince out. David snapped a leash onto his collar, and they began to walk him around the service station.

A friendly-looking man was filling his car as they passed. "Hey, little girl," he called to Christina, who was holding the leash, "are you leading that dog, or is he leading you?"

Prince went over to the man, taking Christina with him. "That's a mighty fine dog!" the man said to David. "Black Lab, isn't he?"

"He's a full-blooded Labrador!" David said proudly. "He'd be worth a lot of money, except that we couldn't get papers on him. A friend of my dad's gave him to us."

"He's a fine dog, with or without papers!" the man said with a grin.

"David! Christina!" Mrs. Patterson called just then, and the kids headed back to the truck. They put Prince back in the camper, then climbed in the cab again with their parents. The motor hummed smoothly as Dad pulled back onto the highway, and everyone settled in for the long trip home.

A little while later the truck was approaching a steep mountain grade, and Mr. Patterson accelerated slightly to help the vehicle up the steep slope. At that instant, a car turned left directly in front of their truck.

Christina screamed. Mr. Patterson responded quickly. He slammed on the brakes and swerved sharply to the left, missing the other vehicle by inches. He swerved back into his own lane, then accelerated hard to regain speed for the mountain grade. He slowly let out his breath as he realized how close they had come to a tragic accident.

* * *

Inside the camper, Prince had been restless and a bit uncomfortable on the swaying floor. He stood up and turned around, and at that moment there was a screech of tires as the camper lurched forward. The sudden movement threw him off balance. The vehicle swerved to one side, throwing him hard against the front of the little LP gas stove, then suddenly lurched again as Mr. Patterson accelerated.

Caught off balance, the big dog fell heavily against the door of the camper, which sprang open as the tremendous bulk of his body hit it. Prince tumbled out the door, landing on the highway behind the camper.

As his body struck the pavement, the big dog tumbled over and over, finally coming to a stop at the white line marking the side of the highway. He raised his head, let out one short yelp, then lay still.

* * *

The camper continued up the highway. The Patterson family were totally unaware of their loss.

"That was a close call," Mom sighed, still trembling. She looked over at her husband. "I'm mighty thankful you were alert and knew how to avoid that accident."

"That was some good driving, Dad!" David agreed.

"I hope Prince is okay," Christina said, concern in her voice.

Mom patted her hand. "I'm sure he's just fine."

They continued up the highway in silence. Several minutes later, Dad noticed headlights in his rearview mirror. The approaching vehicle pulled out as if to pass, then swung back into the lane behind the camper. The driver flashed his brights several times. "I wonder what he wants," Dad muttered.

The vehicle again pulled out to the left, flashed his brights several times, then pulled back in behind. "I wish he'd just pass us," Dad said.

"Maybe it's the police," David suggested.

Dad shook his head. "It doesn't look like a trooper's car," he replied. "Anyway, he'd use his lights if he wanted to pull us over."

The camper came to another steep grade, and the highway widened where the truck lane began.

"Good!" Dad said as he steered the Ford into the right lane. "This guy can pass us now. He has all the room in the world."

The other car pulled up alongside the camper, and

the driver honked his horn several times. "What in the world does he want?" Mr. Patterson fumed.

A woman on the passenger side of the car rolled down the window, pointed to the rear of the camper and shouted. Dad rolled down his window, and the woman shouted again, still pointing to the rear of the Patterson truck, but her words were lost in the noise of the wind. The woman rolled up her window, and the car pulled ahead.

Mr. Patterson flipped on his turn signal and pulled to the side of the highway. "Maybe they were trying to tell us that something's wrong with the truck," he told his family. "I'm gonna check it out." He opened the door, lowered his crutches to the gravel and got out of the truck.

"I hope Prince is all right," Christina said.

Mrs. Patterson squeezed her hand. "I'm sure he's just fine," she reassured her little daughter. "You can see him when we get home."

At that moment, Dad opened the door of the truck. His face looked pale and worried in the dim light from the cab lamp. "The door of the camper was open," he said simply. "Prince is gone!"

Chapter 5
THE SEARCH

Mrs. Patterson stared at her husband. "Prince is gone?" she echoed. "How could he be gone? The children put him in the camper at the service station, just a few minutes ago!"

"When I got to the rear of the camper, the door was open," Dad replied. "Apparently that was what the other driver was trying to tell us. Prince must have fallen out!"

Christina began to cry, and David found himself trying to blink back tears. "Can we find him, Dad?" he asked.

Mr. Patterson looked at him tenderly. "We'll give it our best, Son," he answered softly.

"I...I hope Prince isn't hurt!" Christina sobbed. "We have to find him!"

Mr. Patterson turned the truck around and began to head north. He drove slowly, with his headlights on high beam. The family silently and eagerly scanned both sides of the highway, hoping for a glimpse of their beloved pet. Mom and Dad glanced at each other, realizing that the search was almost certain to be futile. Prince might very well be dead.

They reached the service station where they had stopped for gas, but saw no sign of Prince. Dad went into the station, but the attendant had not seen the huge dog. When he climbed back into the cab of the truck, the entire family sat in silence.

"Help us, Father, to find Prince," Dad prayed aloud. "We don't know what happened, and we don't even know where to look. Help us find him, please. We need Your help. In Jesus' name. Amen." Tears streamed down all four faces.

The Patterson camper pulled back onto the highway and headed south. Again four pairs of eyes watched intently, but finally they reached the spot where Dad had pulled the truck to the side of the road. He pulled over again and sat quietly, thinking.

Finally he spoke in a husky voice. "We're not going home tonight," he told his heartbroken family. "We'll get a motel room for the night, then start searching again in the morning. It'll be light then. We'll find him."

He drove to a nearby motel. A short while later, the family was bedded down for the night, each alone with his own melancholy thoughts of Prince. Christina drifted off to sleep, whispering, "Dear God, please bring my Prince back. Please bring him back."

* * *

The big dog lay beside the highway for several minutes, stunned by the fall from the camper. Finally he struggled to his feet, looked around, and began limping along the highway. Prince was lost, but he was eager to find his family, and instinct told him to head south.

Although the vehicle had been traveling at a rather high speed when Prince fell, he had not sustained any major injuries. One foreleg was slightly sprained, and he favored it a little as he walked; but, miraculously, he was not seriously hurt.

The highway crossed a small creek. Prince left the roadway and made his way to the water's edge for a long drink, then trotted back to the highway again, still heading south. The dog was puzzled as to why the family had left him, but he would find them again. He belonged to them, and they belonged to him.

The long, dark hours of the night passed slowly as the huge dog traveled painfully along the edge of the highway. He simply followed his instincts, and they told him to head south. Just as the rising sun was painting the eastern skies with brilliant hues of orange and crimson, Prince passed by a little motel on the edge of the highway. A traveler slammed a car door, and the sound caught the tired dog's attention.

He turned toward the motel, then suddenly gave a joyful bark. One of the vehicles—a pickup camper—was very familiar.

Sniffing at the wheels of the vehicle, Prince confirmed that it was indeed the Patterson camper. He had found his family! He barked again, joyfully, then stood at the camper door, tail wagging in expectation, waiting for the Pattersons to come out and greet him.

* * *

Inside the motel room, Christina was waiting in line for the bathroom. Suddenly a familiar sound from the parking lot caught her attention, and she ran to the window. She ducked under the curtains and popped her head up where she could see the camper. Her blue eyes widened in delight, and she ducked back out of the curtains, screaming the news of her discovery.

"Daddy!" she yelled, pounding on the bathroom door where her father was shaving. "Come quick! Prince is here! Prince is here! Oh, goody! I knew he'd find us!"

The exuberant little girl began to pound on the door of the closet where her mother was dressing. "Mommy! Prince is here! I asked Jesus to bring him back, and He did!"

Both doors popped open just a crack, and two startled parents observed the little girl dancing about in delight. "Mommy! Daddy!" she shrieked. "Prince is here! He's by the camper!" Mr. Patterson grabbed a bathrobe and his crutches and hurried to the door of the motel room.

* * *

A long, sleek, black limousine was slowly pulling from the parking lot when the pudgy little man in the back seat suddenly leaned forward and tapped the driver on the shoulder. "Stop the car, Parsons!"

The luxurious car slowed to a stop, and the driver turned to see what his employer wanted. "Parsons, look at that magnificent animal!" the chubby man said breathlessly, pointing to Prince, who was sniffing at the door of the camper. "What is he? He's huge!"

"He's a Labrador retriever, sir," the driver responded. "As fine a Labrador as I've ever seen!"

"I know that!" the man in back answered impatiently. "But is he blooded? Could we show him?"

Parsons turned an expert eye back to the dog and studied him critically. "There's a good chance he's a purebred, sir. But, of course, he wouldn't show without papers!"

The wealthy man studied the dog for a moment

with a greedy eye, then turned and scanned the still quiet parking lot of the motel. He opened the back door of the limousine. "Quickly, Parsons, I want him!" He rubbed his pudgy hands together in his excitement. "Hurry, man, I want that dog!"

Parsons reluctantly climbed from the car and called to the dog, which readily came to him. "He has a collar, sir!"

The fat man waved one hand impatiently. "Forget the collar, Parsons! Just get the dog in the car! Move!"

The big, kindly-looking driver started to protest but was stopped by a fierce gleam that suddenly appeared in his boss' eyes. Meekly he took the huge dog by the collar and led him to the back door of the waiting car. At his urging, Prince obediently climbed into the back seat and lay down on the floor. Two car doors slammed, and the big limousine rolled quickly toward the highway.

* * *

Inside the motel room, Mr. Patterson fumbled with the door locks. He finally got them unlatched and flung open the door. Christina followed eagerly onto the sidewalk, her pale green nightgown fluttering in the gentle morning breeze.

Her father frowned, studying the parking lot with a

puzzled look. He turned to his daughter. "Where is he, Sweetheart?"

The little girl ran around behind the camper. "He was right here, Daddy! He was barking and barking and looking up at the camper like he wanted us to open the door! I saw him!"

The tall professor pursed his lips and gave a loud whistle. "Here, Prince!" he called. "Prince! Here, boy!"

Neither of the Pattersons noticed the long, black limousine as it accelerated onto the highway.

Chapter 6

JONATHAN ABBOT

Jonathan Abbot was a very wealthy man. Heir to the Western States Steel fortune and owner of numerous properties in several states, he was known throughout much of the West as somewhat of a miser. Although he was one of the wealthiest men in the state, no one would have suspected it by his appearance. Usually shabbily dressed, Mr. Abbot thought nothing of spending large amounts of money on his cars or his dogs, but he didn't give a second thought to his wardrobe.

Middle-aged, short and fat, he held memberships in the most exclusive of lodges and country clubs, but had no real friends. Rumor was that in earlier years he had been engaged to the beautiful daughter of the governor, but that she had spurned him for another man, and he had never married. He and three servants lived at Ironwood, a rambling, sixty-room brownstone mansion just north of Silverton, Washington.

Abbot fancied himself as something of a dog expert. His money had procured some of the finest show dogs in the country, and the ribbons and trophies adorning the teakwood walls of his den were silent testimony to the fact that the kennels at Ironwood did house some champions; but the arrogant little man knew nothing about dogs. Parsons, the chauffeur, was actually his trainer and handler, and the success of the Abbot kennels really belonged to him. The pair were returning from a regional in which one of Abbot's setters had taken a number of awards, including Best of Show.

Michael Parsons was just the opposite of his selfish employer. Tall and good-natured, he was an immaculate dresser, and spent most of his meager salary on clothing. His meals and lodging were provided for him at Ironwood. Like Abbot, he had never married. An expert dog handler, he had spent the last eighteen years in the employ of Mr. Abbot. Although the salary was small and the working relationship with the eccentric tycoon was far from ideal, Parsons had cherished his position as Mr. Abbot's trainer simply because it afforded him the opportunity to work with some of the finest dogs in the world.

Mr. Abbot, on the other hand, cared nothing for the dogs themselves; they were simply a means to an end. He collected dogs in much the same way that other wealthy men collect guns or cars. To him, the animals were merely showpieces. His chief pleasure in life was to win at the shows, to prove to the world that his collection of dogs was superior to that of his competitors.

Prince lay on the carpeted floor of the big car. Abbot was seated across from him, and the huge, friendly dog made a couple of advances toward him, but was sternly rebuffed. Finally, the Labrador lay quietly.

Parsons glanced in the rearview mirror and observed Mr. Abbot studying the brass nameplate on the red leather collar he had taken from the dog. While he watched, the man stuffed the collar under the thick, cushioned seat of the limousine.

Late that evening, the magnificent car purred to a stop in front of a pair of wrought iron gates. In the rear seat Mr. Abbot glanced at his watch, scowling as he read the time. "I should have driven myself," he muttered. "We should have been here an hour ago!"

"We could have flown, sir."

"Watch it, Parsons!" Mr. Abbot snapped. "You know how I feel about flying."

Parsons lowered the car window, inserted a key in the box beside the driveway, then drove through the massive gates as they swung open. The gates closed quietly behind the big car.

Ironwood, nestled in the foothills of the Cascade Mountains, was a hideaway paradise. Three thousand secluded acres of rugged hills, crystal-clear creeks, and small, cattail-fringed lakes were enclosed within the six-foot brick walls that ran the entire perimeter of the property. Emerald green lawns surrounded the hilltop mansion, as well as the riding stables and kennels behind it, and dozens of elegant peacocks roamed the grounds.

Parsons drove up the circular drive in front of the mansion, and a servant appeared to help Mr. Abbot with his luggage. The tall chauffeur assisted with the unloading, then closed the trunk of the limousine. He turned and faced Mr. Abbot.

"With your permission, sir, I'll get the dog settled in his new kennel. Then I'll meet the train at the station. The other dogs are due shortly."

"Very well." Abbot nodded, then turned and walked into the house.

Parsons parked the limousine in the twelve-car garage, then got a large collar and a leash from the grooming area. He opened the back door of the car and knelt on the cement as he fastened the collar around Prince's massive neck. Snapping the leash to the collar, he stood up and whistled the dog out of the car.

Prince stood just outside the garage door stretching

and surveying the unfamiliar surroundings. The tall trainer knelt again beside him and ran expert hands over the dog, noting with satisfaction the proud head, the huge chest and the strong but graceful legs. "You'll show well, Lad," he told the dog. "Mark my word, you'll soon be winning ribbons to grace the Abbot kennels."

He examined the injured leg, then wrapped it expertly with tape. "Just for a day or two," he promised the dog. "It ain't hurt bad." The gentle man talked softly to the big dog as he quickly brushed his coat, then led him to a clean, empty kennel. Prince quickly sensed in Parsons a man who could be trusted.

"This here's your new home, Lad," he told Prince, as he unsnapped the leash. "Hope you like it." As Prince examined the enclosure, Parsons prepared a bed, food and fresh water. The man spent a few more minutes with the dog, stroking his head and talking to him in a soothing voice. As he turned to go, Prince held out his right front paw.

Parsons chuckled at the gesture. "Decided to be friends already, have you?" he said, smiling. "That's good! You and I are gonna get along just fine!" Then he took the huge paw and shook it solemnly.

As the van backed out of the garage, Prince stood

watching at the door of his kennel. When Parsons had driven away, he walked to the rear of the kennel, sniffed at the clean blanket carefully placed atop a bed of fresh-smelling straw, then sighed deeply as he lay down and closed his eyes. Within minutes, the tired dog was asleep.

More than a thousand miles to the south, a little girl cried herself to sleep.

Chapter 7

THE JOURNEY BEGINS

Sunlight streamed in the kitchen window, blazing a pattern of golden squares on the linoleum as the Pattersons sat down to Sunday breakfast. Mr. Patterson looked at the somber faces around him. The family was unusually quiet, and he knew without asking that the missing Prince was foremost on each mind.

"Would you ask the blessing, Christina?" he suggested quietly.

"Dear God," the little girl began, "thank You for our food. Thank You for Mommy and Daddy and David." Suddenly she was in tears. "Please, God, would You give our Prince back to us. He's lost, God, but You know where he is. Help him not to be hungry, and help him to know that we miss him."

Christina looked up at her father with a triumphant smile on her face. "God's gonna bring Prince home, Daddy!" she said brightly. "I just know it!" Mr. and Mrs. Patterson looked at each other. Mrs. Patterson wiped tears from her eyes.

* * *

Monday evening Mr. Abbot found his trainer in

the kennel exercise yard. Prince sat quietly beside him. "How's he coming, Parsons?"

"Just fine, sir," the tall man answered. "But we still can't show him without papers."

Mr. Abbott suddenly caught sight of the bandaged leg and glanced up quickly at the trainer. "What's wrong with the leg?" he asked sharply.

Parsons shrugged slightly. "Just a slight sprain, sir. It's really nothing. It's my guess that he took a fall, perhaps from an auto."

The wealthy man stooped over, examining the bandage from a distance. "Will he still show?"

"The leg is fine, sir; really it is," Parsons assured him. "I'll have the bandages off in a day or two. But we still cannot show him without papers."

Abbot grinned triumphantly. He pulled a sheaf of papers from his rumpled suit coat and thrust them suddenly at his trainer. "Here," he exclaimed, "let's not hear anything more about papers. This dog has his."

Parsons unfolded the documents and read them in disbelief. "Prince Edward III," he read aloud. He then noted the name of the sire and dam on the certificate. "These are both champions!"

Abbot nodded, immensely pleased with himself.

"Prince Edward comes from good stock," he said. "He hails from a long line of British champions. His papers are perfectly in order, and unless someone questions his registration, the British kennels will never know."

The tall trainer frowned, his disgust written openly across his features. He viewed the deceitful actions of his employer with undisguised contempt.

Abbot's eyes suddenly narrowed, and he gave the trainer a hard look. "Parsons, if anyone ever questions Prince Edward's credentials, you will no longer be in my employ, and you'll have no pension. Do you get my meaning? If anyone should ask, we had Prince flown from London just a few weeks ago."

Parsons nodded uncomfortably. "Very well, sir."

The training of Prince consumed much of Parsons' time during the next few weeks. Each morning after exercising and caring for the other dogs, he would spend several hours working with the big Labrador, training him for the shows. Prince was an apt pupil, and he learned quickly. Michael Parsons, the dog expert, was developing another champion.

The restlessness of the big dog bothered the trainer. Whenever Parsons could slip into the kennel area without Prince's sensing his presence, he would always find the dog at the far end of the enclosure pacing restlessly back and forth, staring longingly toward the south. During the workouts, the Labrador obeyed readily enough, but the sensitive trainer realized that the dog's heart was not in the work.

The image of a little blonde girl standing beside a tall, thin man on crutches in a motel parking lot still troubled him as well. He could still see her worried little face reflected in the rearview mirror of the limousine.

Two months after Prince came to Ironwood, he entered his first dog show. As Parsons put him expertly through his paces, Prince responded readily enough, but he seemed to the trainer to be stiff and distant. The tall man again sensed that the big dog's heart wasn't in it. He just didn't carry himself like a champion.

Abbot stood beside the limousine after the show, staring at the pale yellow ribbon in his hand. "Third place?" he screamed. "No Abbot entry takes third place! Never again, Parsons! Never again!"

The little man clutched his program until his knuckles turned white. "The dog is a champion, Parsons! Why don't you show him like one? That's what I'm paying you for, man!"

* * *

Three days later the sun was dipping low in the West when Prince trotted quietly across the manicured lawns. The door to his kennel had somehow been left unlatched, and the restless dog had been quick to discover his opportunity for escape.

When he reached the gate of the Abbot estate a moment later, the animal lay down on his belly and wriggled under the wrought iron barrier. As he passed under the gate, the shiny brass collar around his neck caught on the decorative piece on the end of one of the vertical bars. Prince twisted and pulled, but the collar held him fast.

The massive Labrador drew back, then lunged against the offending collar with all his weight. The buckle on the collar snapped under the sudden strain. The heavy collar flew through the air, landed on the asphalt with a dull clang, then rolled down the driveway, finally coming to rest in the aloes at the bottom of the hill. Prince scrambled under the gate, and suddenly he was free!

The big dog trotted to the edge of the woods, paused for a moment and looked back, then entered the woods at a trot. He was heading south. The long journey had begun.

Chapter 8
THUNDER

Prince emerged from the woods just as the sun was peeking over the oak-shrouded ridges to the east. The effortless, mile-consuming gait with which he had started was gone, and it had been replaced by the stumbling, careless shuffle of an exhausted animal.

The big dog had covered just over a hundred miles in three days. He had been traveling due south, and his route had taken him through some rugged country. For three days he had been fighting his way through tangles of briars, wading or swimming across creeks and rivers, and climbing over steep mountains and through deep valleys. Creeks and ponds along the way had furnished him with plenty of water, but he had not eaten since he left Ironwood. Prince was tired, lonely and very hungry.

He stood on the side of a steep hill, surveying the scene before him. A small, weatherbeaten farm was nestled in the emerald green valley below. An elderly man was attempting to drive a small herd of cattle through a narrow gate into a steep pasture area. Prince sat down on the hillside above and watched.

The man drove the cattle along the edge of a sagging fence perpendicular to the faded red barn. But he ran into trouble when the big, rangy animals reached the gate. Half of the herd had passed through without incident, but one stubborn old milker balked when she reached it. She turned and loped back toward the coolness of the barn. When the old farmer turned to cut her off, the rest of the herd reversed direction and stampeded toward the barn also.

The old man tried three more times. Each time the same stubborn cow was causing him grief. Each time she reached the gate she would suddenly bolt back to the barn, and the rest of the herd would follow. The fourth time the herd came charging back, the tired, frustrated farmer was able to get between some of the cattle and the barn and head them off ahead of time. But as the herd turned, several of the animals stumbled against the edge of a gate leading into a pen adjacent to the barn. The pen held a mean-tempered black Angus bull named Thunder. The gate swung open, and suddenly Thunder was free.

The old farmer didn't realize that the big bull was loose. He turned toward the barn, shaking his fist at the cattle inside. "Y'all not git the best of me!" he shouted. "If I'm not smarter than the lot of ye, ya might as well be rennin' the farm 'stead of me!"

As he neared the barn, he turned, hearing the

sound of heavy hooves. He gave a sudden cry of fear as, in a flash, the fierce bull was upon him.

Thunder charged the man, intent on goring him with one of his wicked-looking horns. The farmer turned and bolted for a five-foot stone wall that butted up against the corner of the barn. He gave a mighty leap, clawed desperately at the top of the wall, then fell back to the earth.

The huge bull struck him just as he landed, knocking him to the loose trampled earth of the cow lot. Rolling clear of the pounding hooves, the man cried for help.

At that instant, Prince came flying down the hillside and cleared the wall in a mighty leap. The man needed his help! Barking and growling fiercely, he charged the angry bull.

By instinct, Prince leaped for the bull's throat. As he struck, his weight and momentum knocked the startled Thunder slightly off balance. The bull turned to meet this new challenger, the man on the ground suddenly forgotten. He swung his head in a vicious lunge at the dog, intending to gut him with one quick thrust of his spearlike horns. But the dog was no longer there. He had leaped to the rear of the bull, and as the bigger animal turned, slashed savagely at his flank. His teeth found their mark, and the bull bellowed in rage and pain. He swung around, pawing the earth, determined to kill the smaller animal that was tormenting him so.

Suddenly Prince appeared on the other side, snarling, slashing, leaping. As he attacked, he moved in and out so fast that the enraged bull was never quite sure where the next assault was coming from.

The farmer had found his feet and had scrambled over the wall to safety. He scurried behind the fence, swung the gate to the bull's pen open again, and called to the dog, "'Ere, boy! Good work! Bring ol' Thunder 'ere! We'll put 'im be'ind bars! Bring 'im 'ere, boy!"

Prince did exactly that. Snarling, snapping, slashing, he drove the confused bovine back into his stall. The farmer swung the heavy gate closed, then heaved the bar into place. "Well done, Lad!" he called to the dog. "Well done!" He knelt and snapped his fingers. "Come 'ere, Lad. Let's get acquainted!"

Prince went to him eagerly. The old man ran strong, gnarled fingers along the back of his head, then along his flanks. "Ya saved my skin, boy!" he said. "I owe ye!" He stroked the big dog gently, scratching his ears, patting his shoulder.

Prince sat down, looked up at the kind old farmer, then gravely put out his right paw. The man laughed at the gesture, then shook the proffered paw. "Glad ta know you, Lad," he said to the dog. "I shore appreci-ate what ya did fer me there! I was a goner fer shore!"

He looked toward the barn. "Think ya can help me get the rest of those wuthless critters back out ta pasture, where they belong? I'll 'elp ye, and we'll do it together."

Prince had never worked cattle before, but he seemed to know instinctively what to do, and in moments the rest of the herd was safely in the pas-ture. The farmer gave him an appreciative glance. "A Labrador that works cattle, eh? That's unusual!"

He studied the dog thoughtfully. "I don't know who ya are, Lad," he remarked, "but ya know yore stuff! Ya act like ya've been around cattle all yore life! Care ta hire on as a cow 'and?"

He stooped and stroked the dog again, then turned toward the little farmhouse with its sagging porch and peeling gray paint. "How 'bout a bit of brea'fast? I don't see a collar on ye. I'm abettin' ya could use a bite to eat!" Prince followed the farmer eagerly, not understanding all his words but enjoying the man's friendly tone.

The man's boots clomped hollowly across the

porch, and the squeaky front door protested as he shoved it open. The man entered, then turned as Prince hesitated. "Come in, Lad, come in!" he encouraged. "Y'all be welcome 'ere!"

He led the big dog into the kitchen, and a plump, pleasant-faced woman turned in astonishment from the wood cookstove. "Amos Elkins," she scolded, "where did you find such an animal?"

The old farmer grinned like a possum eating poke-berries. "Martha," he said politely, as if he were about to introduce royalty, "I want ya ta meet a friend of mine. Don't know 'is name yet, but I owe 'im aplenty. 'E just saved ma skin. I want ya ta feed 'im like 'e was the guv'nor."

He turned to Prince. "Lad, this 'ere's the Missus, and she'll welcome ya just like I do, even though she may growl at ya at first. But she's a kind ol' soul, and she'll fix the best vittles ya would ever care to sink yore teeth inta."

The woman gave a playful swat at her husband with a tattered potholder, then turned her attention back to the cast-iron skillet on the stove. She tried to look stern, but the old man had caught the twinkle in her eye, and he knew that his case was already won.

"Where'd he come from?" she asked, stirring the gravy.

Amos took a pot from its hook on the wall, filled it with water from a bucket on the sideboard, and set it on the floor for Prince. He filled a Bell jar with water from the same bucket, then sat down at the table and took a deep swig before answering. "I think my guardin' angel sent 'im," he answered soberly. He told her the story of the close call with Thunder, making sure that she realized that she would be the Widow Elkins were it not for the big dog.

She saw immediately what he was leading up to and did her best to get her defenses up in time. "Amos," she argued, "we're barely making it as it is now! How do you expect to be able to feed a critter as big as he is?"

The old man shrugged, and his wrinkled features softened into a huge smile as he watched Prince empty the pan of water. He filled the pan again, then turned back to the woman. "Don't rightly know, Martha," he said finally. "But I owe the pup. 'E saved ma skin. I plan ta keep 'im, and feed 'im, even if it means I go 'ungry. We'll manage."

"But he belongs to somebody!" the old woman argued, knowing all the while that she had already lost the battle. "They'll come alookin' fer him!"

Amos shook his white head. "Not ta anybody around 'ere, 'e don't. I figger 'e's a right valuable dog. Who do we know what could afford such a critter? 'E ain't from around 'ere."

He stepped closer to the big dog. "Look at 'is coat, Martha. Ya can see 'ow 'e's been taken care of. But 'is coat is matted now, and 'e's picked up some burrs. I say the dog 'as been travelin' a good ways."

He knelt beside Prince and lifted one paw. "Look at 'is pads, Martha. They's all cut and worn. 'E's been travelin', and 'is feet just ain't used ta it. I say 'e's ours."

The woman shook her head, realizing that, as usual, she had lost the argument. Amos Elkins would have his way. He planned to keep the gigantic dog, and she knew it was useless to try to talk him out of it. She smoothed her apron, then turned back to the stove. "Well, wash up, Amos," she said. "Breakfast is ready."

Chapter 9

ON THE ROAD AGAIN

Amos and Martha Elkins sat at the tiny kitchen table, Martha with her usual cup of tea, Amos gulping his routine breakfast of two fried eggs, biscuits and gravy. Today the old man's attention was not on Martha's cooking. He ate without even tasting the food.

"Look at 'im eat, Martha!" he cackled. "The way 'e's beltin' through the vittles, ya'd think 'e 'adn't eaten in two days!"

Martha nodded soberly. "I imagine he eats like that all the time, Amos," she answered. "Just look at the size of him!"

The pot on the floor in front of Prince held biscuits and gravy and two fried eggs, while a second pot held a generous portion of leftover stew. In minutes, the big dog had emptied them both. The kind old farmer refilled the one pot with the last of the stew.

Martha sighed deeply. "He's et our supper."

But Amos wasn't worried. "There's nearly a 'ole side of beef in the freezer," he pointed out. "And I'll pick ya a mess of fresh vegetables from the garden. Ya can make another stew."

The old man regarded Prince with an appreciative eye. "Martha," he said, "doesn't 'e kinda remind ya of Shep?"

Martha glanced at the dog, then back at her husband. "Shep weren't nearly that big."

"I know, I know," the man agreed. "But still, don't 'e remind ya of Shep?"

She shrugged. "Maybe."

"Look at 'im," he persisted. "The way 'e 'olds 'is 'ead, the way 'e gulps 'is food, the way 'e looks at us. I say 'e's a lot like Shep. And Shep were the best farm dog ever was."

Martha dropped her empty cup on the table with a clatter and raised her hands in mock surrender. "Amos Elkins," she said resignedly, "you shoulda been a salesman instead of a farmer. You just don't give up, do ye? You can keep the dog. I ain't gonna raise a ruckus over him. But I still don't know how we can ever hope to feed him. I'll bet he eats three times what Shep did."

Grinning from ear to ear, Amos reached over and tenderly patted her arm. He suddenly stood up, walked over to Prince and knelt beside him. "Why are ya favorin' that one paw?" he asked. "Let me see it."

He gently raised Prince's left front paw, then

shook his head as he turned the foot and saw the pad. "The poor chap's got a thorn, Martha," he said. "Looks like it's afesterin' bad. I'll see if 'e'll let me get it out fer 'im." He drew a Barlow knife from the pocket of his overalls.

Several minutes later, after the noxious thorn had been removed and the wound, salved and bandaged, the kind farmer began to rub salve on the dog's three other raw pads. "This'll fix ya up in no time," he told Prince. "These feet of yourn look pretty ragged."

Prince fell asleep on the kitchen floor. After Amos had headed for the fields, Martha got a short, three-legged stool from the pantry and sat quietly beside the sleeping animal. She gently rubbed his head and scratched his ears. Amos was right. Although it would be tough to feed such a large animal, it would be good to have a dog around again. Shep had been dead for nearly three years.

The Labrador slept all day, waking only once to drink from the pan of water and gulp a plate of food that Martha offered. That evening Amos came and fetched him before he headed for the pasture.

"Time to bring in the cattle," he told the dog as they walked up the steep hillside. "I kinda figger that with ya 'ere, even ol' Angie won't dare kick up much of a fuss."

The old man was right. The cantankerous old cow tried once or twice to head the herd in a deviant direction, but the snarling, snapping Prince quickly changed her mind. By the second evening of Prince's stay, she had learned simply to follow the rest of the herd placidly. The third evening Amos sent Prince to the pasture alone to bring in the cows.

The gentle old farmer rubbed the soothing salve on the dog's feet twice each day, and they were healing nicely. Two generous meals a day, combined with skillful brushings and a lot of personal attention, restored the giant dog to his former magnificent appearance.

Prince had found a good home, had he wanted it. But in spite of the loving attention and generous care heaped upon him by the old couple, his heart was calling him away. A little blonde-haired girl and a dark-haired boy needed him. His home was with the Pattersons. He couldn't rest until he found them again. He must head south.

As much as he hated to admit it to himself, Amos Elkins finally realized the signs. As the dog grew rested and healthy, he also grew restless. The old farmer had no idea to whom "Lad" belonged, but he knew dogs well enough to realize that the magnificent animal would never really belong to him. The dog had another love, and it would be only right to allow him to respond to it.

After supper one evening, Amos called Prince to him and tenderly scratched the dog's head for several minutes. With a sigh he led the Labrador to the front gate, opened it, and led him into the road.

"Take the road, Lad," he said in a husky voice. "I know yore not really ourn. Somewhere out there somebody's awaitin' for ye, and yore just awaitin' to git to them. I shoulda seen it afore. Go 'ome, Lad."

Prince took two steps down the road, then turned and looked up at the man, his head cocked to one side. Amos waved him on. "Go on, Lad," he called. "It's all right. Martha and me'll git along without ya."

Prince took one last look, then trotted down the road, again heading south. There were tears in the old man's eyes as he closed the gate.

* * *

Alice Patterson smiled as she watched Christina through the front window. The girl was sprawled in the porch swing, gently rocking herself back and forth with one foot. A teddy bear was clutched to her heart. Her mother sighed. The loss of Prince had been a difficult burden for the little six-year-old to bear, but finally she appeared to be getting over it.

As Mrs. Patterson watched, Christina was smiling and chattering to her bear. Her mother slipped over to the screen door, out of sight, but where she could hear the little girl's words.

The smile froze on the mother's lips. "And when Prince comes home, Teddy," the childish voice floated into the house, "we're gonna have a big party! It'll be like the progidal…like the proj…like the son that ran away. We'll have a welcome home party! There'll be cupcakes for you and me and David, and a big bone and a whole bag of dog food for Prince, and we'll all live happily ever after."

A soft sigh escaped the girl, and a lump came to her mother's throat. "I hope Prince gets here soon," the little voice continued.

Mrs. Patterson quietly opened the screen door and slipped out onto the porch. She lifted Christina's feet and sat down on the end of the porch swing. "Honey," she said gently, "I think you and I need to have a talk."

Christina sat upright, then snuggled up against her mother. "Okay, Mommy," she agreed, "about what?"

The woman searched desperately for the right words. "Honey," she said gently, "Prince has been gone for over two months."

The little girl nodded. "Do you think he'll be here soon, Mommy?"

Her mother took both of Christina's hands in hers. "Sweetheart," she sighed, "I don't think we'll ever see Prince again. It's been too long, Honey. He might be living with another family, or he might have even gotten..." She stopped, not daring to say the next word.

"But Mommy, Prince will come home!" Christina insisted. "I know he will! If he's living with somebody else, he'll leave them and come to us! I know he will!"

Mrs. Patterson breathed a silent prayer: *Help me, Father, to say this without hurting her. She wants him back so badly!*

She took a deep breath. "Christina," she said slowly, "Prince has been gone a long, long time. If he were going to come home, I think he would have been here by now. I...I just don't think we're going to see him again. I'm afraid he's gone for good."

The little girl's lower lip began to tremble. "But I asked Jesus to bring Prince back, Mommy! And I believe He will!"

Mrs. Patterson gently stroked Christina's hair. "But

we don't always get what we pray for, Sweetheart."

"But I asked in Jesus' name, Mommy. My memory verse says, 'If ye shall ask any thing in my name, I will do it.' That's John 14:14. We learned it in Sunday school."

"Yes, Sweetheart, but…"

"Do you believe that Jesus can bring him back, Mommy? Do you?"

"Yes, Christina, but Prince has been gone so long! And we don't know where he is, and…"

"You don't believe it, do you, Mommy? You don't. But I do! Jesus knows where Prince is, and He knows where I live, and He's gonna bring him home to me! He is! I know He is!"

David leaned his bicycle against the front steps just then and came bounding up onto the porch. "Don't be stupid, Christina," he said cruelly. "Prince isn't ever coming back! He's probably dead by now!" He slammed the screen door as he hurried into the house.

The little girl jumped from the porch swing and dashed down the steps. "Prince is coming back!" she cried. "He's not dead! He's not! And he's gonna come back! Jesus will bring him back! You'll see!" Sobbing, she ran into the backyard.

Chapter 10

HUNGRY

The next morning found Prince on the outskirts of a small town. The aroma of baking bread wafted out from a small bakery, and Prince sniffed the air hungrily. He sat at the door of the bakery for nearly ten minutes, hoping that some kind human being would appear and offer him a meal. But the meal never materialized, and finally the hungry dog began to wander through town.

Cutting through a back alley, he again caught the smell of food. He followed the scent until it led him into the backyard of a shabby, dilapidated house. Sheets on the line billowed in the breeze like sails to the wind, and the yard was cluttered with trash and two or three old vehicles. At the back stoop, a tired-looking German shepherd was gulping a large bowlful of dog food mixed with hot table scraps.

Prince moved right in. The shepherd turned and growled a warning, but Prince bared his teeth in a snarl, and the smaller dog quickly backed down. He retreated to the end of his chain and sulkily watched as the Labrador devoured his food. Prince had nearly finished when the back door of the house suddenly opened and a woman's voice filled the air with curses. Prince looked up just as a brick struck him in the shoulder. He hastily retreated from the yard.

"You mangy, good-for-nothing thief!" the woman screamed. "How dare you come into our yard and eat Duke's food!" And then the curses rang out again. Prince trotted quickly down the alley. A few minutes later he left the little town behind him. He was still hungry.

That afternoon he drank greedily from a clear, swift stream as it tumbled and splashed down the mountainside. His thirst quenched, his thoughts turned again to food. He charged into a shallow pool and snapped at the brook trout darting about, but they were much too fast for him. All he got was one mouthful of water after another. He followed the stream from pool to pool, but the results were always the same. He simply was no match for the lively trout.

As he left the banks of the creek and headed uphill, he suddenly caught the scent of another animal. Crouching low, he rounded a bush to come face-to-face with a coyote. The other animal had made a kill and was just starting to devour the lifeless rabbit pinned beneath his paw. When he saw Prince, the coyote snarled in defiance.

Prince charged, fangs bared, and the other animal deserted the kill and ran for the safety of the hillside. Once he was satisfied that the coyote was gone, the dog returned to the rabbit and finished the coyote's meal.

It was Prince's first experience with nature's way of supplying food in the wild, and it taught the dog a valuable lesson. Previously, food had always been provided in a dish or bowl, but the big dog was learning that food also came in other forms. When a rabbit flashed across his path a few minutes later, the Labrador instantly gave chase. But the rabbit had too much of a head start and was safely in his burrow before the big dog could catch up with him.

Later that evening, however, Prince stalked and caught his first rabbit. He was quickly learning the ways of the wild. He would have to, if he were to survive the journey that still lay ahead.

Chapter 11
MAD DOG!

A meadowlark high in a white oak sang a cheery morning song as Prince entered the town of Redmond. He was now in Oregon. He had spent several days in the wild but was none the worse for the experience. He now knew how to find his own food, and he had eaten fairly well. He had thinned Oregon's rabbit population slightly and had taken an occasional unwary grouse or ground squirrel by surprise. On one occasion, he had driven an entire pack of wild dogs from the young deer they had just killed. He had feasted royally while the pack snarled and complained from a respectful distance.

The pads of his feet had given him no more trouble. Amos Elkins' salve had worked wonders, and the feet were now toughened and in good condition for the rigors of the long journey. He was now in top physical shape, and each day put a good number of miles behind him.

But another need had arisen. He desperately missed human companionship. The longing that drove him ever southward was for the Patterson family, but as he entered town, he was just looking to be with people—any people. The big, friendly Labrador loved human company.

The chatter of young voices caught his attention, and he crossed the street and entered a city park. It was Saturday morning, and a group of children were swarming noisily over the slides, merry-go-round and swing sets. Three young mothers sat on the benches nearby, tending infants in strollers and complaining about the price of groceries. Prince paused to drink from a puddle at the edge of the sidewalk, then trotted eagerly toward the children.

Several boys were playing freeze tag among the tall eucalyptus trees lining the edge of the playground. With a bark of joy, Prince ran forward to join in the game. He leaped up on a youngster, licking his face.

The boy was terrified as the gigantic dog lunged for him. Screaming in fear, he whirled around and fell to the ground. He covered his face with his arms to ward off what he perceived as a vicious attack.

Hearing his screams, one of the mothers on the bench leaped to her feet. She dashed across the park lawn toward her son who was cowering on the ground in fear. Her heart pounded as she saw the huge animal towering over the form of her son. Her screams filled the park. The children on the swings and slides suddenly grew quiet.

A police car was cruising by the park at just that

moment, and the woman's screams arrested the attention of the young officer at the wheel. He swerved the patrol car sharply across the street and ran the vehicle right up on the sidewalk. He and his partner dashed through the park toward the screaming woman.

As they passed the benches, the two mothers pointed and screamed. "It's a mad dog!" one of them shrilled. "It's attacking the children!" The officers both drew their revolvers.

When the policemen were still thirty or forty yards from the scene, Prince suddenly whirled and dashed toward another terrified child. Still unaware that his size was a fearful thing to the children, he simply wanted to play. As he bounded toward the second boy, the officers opened fire.

A forty-five-caliber bullet caught Prince in the hip, knocking him off his feet. He tumbled onto the ground, then sprang to his feet, facing the officers in bewilderment. They both fired again, and a second bullet creased the side of the big dog's face. He flinched in pain, then turned and dashed for the cover of nearby bushes. Several more shots rang out, and bullets splatted into the earth just inches from where he lay. He crawled out of the bushes on the side away from the officers and raced for the safety of a small building.

As Prince ran behind the park rest rooms, the two officers stopped to reload. One officer ran for his car to radio for help, while the second frantically attempted to evacuate the young mothers and children from the area. "Get out of the park!" he shouted. "It's a mad dog! Run to the police car!" In seconds the playground was abandoned as mothers and children scurried to safety. The officer ran into the center of the street to halt traffic, then ushered the panicking group across to the safety of the shops lining the street.

The other patrolman was on his police radio. "All available cars to Warner Park!" he called into the microphone. "We have a mad dog on the loose! A number of children's lives are at stake! I repeat—a mad dog is loose in Warner Park. Officers need assistance!"

When the cry "mad dog" is uttered, fear spreads through a crowd like a plague. In minutes, four patrol cars were parked at the curb, their lights flashing a red and blue panic message. The officers assembled on the sidewalk with rifles, shotguns and revolvers drawn and ready. A throng of men armed with shovels, axes and hayrakes from the hardware store across the street stood on the sidewalk, ready to assist the policemen. This "mad dog" would not escape! Across the street the crowd of spectators on the sidewalk now numbered in the hundreds.

The chief of police was there in person to direct the assault on the "mad dog." He ordered his men to spread out in a wide pattern, then instructed the civilian volunteers to surround the perimeter of the park with their makeshift weapons.

Prince lay in the bushes behind the rest rooms, licking his wounded hip, which was still bleeding slightly and was now throbbing painfully. The big dog was confused and hurt. He had sought companionship from these people who looked friendly, but they had shot at him and hurt him.

Once the volunteers were in place around the perimeter of the park, the officers moved in toward the rest rooms with their guns cocked and ready. Had they had the chance to surround the bushes where Prince lay hidden, the big dog would have been shot to death right there in the park. But as they advanced, one of the officers thought he saw a flash of movement, and he fired a volley of shots into the bushes. His target was the bush right next to the one where Prince lay hidden, and the shots alarmed the wounded dog. He dashed from the bushes directly toward the line of civilians at the edge of the park grounds.

Several policemen threw their weapons into firing position, but an authoritative voice rang out. "Hold your fire, men!" the chief ordered. "Too many civilians in the line of fire!"

Some of the men swung their assorted weapons at the big dog as he raced by, but wounded as he was, Prince was still able to dodge and maneuver through the line. He was now safely out of the park. Then he made a tragic mistake.

An officer reached the edge of the park just then and fired a hasty shot at the fleeing dog. Prince turned and dashed through a gate and began to limp between rows of big trucks and heavy equipment, looking desperately for a hiding place. He had just entered the city vehicle maintenance yards. The spot offered many excellent hiding places, but the entire property was surrounded by a seven-foot chain link fence. The officer who had fired the shot came running up and quickly closed the two wide gates.

"We have him now!" he shouted to the others. "This gate is the only way out!"

Prince was trapped, completely at the mercy of a group of armed men who were determined to kill him to protect their children.

Chapter 12
JERRY JACKSON

Jerry Jackson had just fueled his big diesel tow truck and backed the huge vehicle in beside the city garage to air up a tire when a mechanic shouted across the yard at him. "Watch out, Jerry!" the man called. "There's a mad dog loose in here somewhere! Get back in your truck!" The mechanic ran into the office and slammed the door.

Jerry was a big, easy-going man who thoroughly enjoyed his work. In his sixteen years with the city, he had not missed a single day of work. He enjoyed a reputation among the city crews as a man who could be depended on in a pinch.

Jerry turned to see the chief of police swing the yard gate open for just an instant to allow a group of heavily armed officers to rush into the yard. The gate was closed again quickly.

They're not taking any chances, the big man thought to himself. He grabbed a three-foot steel wrecking bar from the back of his tow truck and scrambled into the safety of his cab. As he watched through the windshield, the police fanned out across the yard, searching between the vehicles and equipment.

Just then a curious sound caught his attention. He cocked his head, listening intently. He heard the same sound again! It sounded like a baby whimpering. Curious, he opened the door of the cab just a few inches and leaned out. The sound seemed to be coming from underneath his tow truck.

Jerry inched the door of the truck open wider and cautiously slid around the side of the cab back to the rear deck of the vehicle, gripping the heavy bar tightly in one hand. He knelt on the deck beside the winch and leaned over as far as he dared, peering into the shade beneath his vehicle.

He saw the source of the strange, barely audible moans. A huge dog was lying underneath the rear axle, licking repeatedly at a bloody wound near his hindquarters. When he saw the big man looking down at him, he whimpered, his big tail thumping softly on the gravel.

This ain't no mad dog! the man told himself. Cautiously, he extended the bar toward the dog. The dog leaned forward and licked it. There was a pleading look in the animal's sad eyes.

Jerry Jackson was a man who knew and loved dogs. As a young boy, his goal was to be a veterinarian when he grew up, but the goal had somehow never been reached. Jerry realized that the huge dog beneath his truck was neither mad nor dangerous, but he was badly hurt. Tossing the steel bar back inside the cab, he knelt down and crawled under the edge of the truck to the dog. He reached out and touched the big Labrador, who feebly licked his fingers.

Jerry crawled back out from under the truck and looked quickly around him. No police officers were in sight, but several shots suddenly rang out from somewhere across the yard. He crawled quickly back to Prince.

"We's gonna hafta move fast, old friend," he told the dog softly. "Iffen they find you, they's gonna shoot you!" Grunting, he dragged the heavy dog out to the edge of the truck, then ran around to the right side and opened the door of the cab. He glanced around quickly to make sure that the officers were not yet in sight, then ran to the rear of the vehicle and struggled to lift the huge dog.

Moments later he slipped the big truck into gear and rumbled toward the closed gates. Prince lay on the floorboard of the truck, panting softly, his eyes closed. "It's gonna take some luck, old friend," the man whispered to the dog as he slowed the truck to a stop in front of the gates.

"Jerry!" a police sergeant called to him, gesturing with his shotgun. "What do you think you're doing? Get that truck back! We've got a mad dog in here!"

Jerry leaned out the window. "Got a call to tow one of our vehicles involved in a minor collision on Highway 97. Can you open the gate for a second to let me slip through? It's urgent!"

The man stared up at him. "Jerry, are you crazy? We got the dog bottled up in here, and he can't escape as long as the gate stays closed."

Jerry frowned. "Get a couple men over here to cover the gate while I hurry through," he suggested.

The sergeant shook his head. "Can't do it, Jerry," he insisted. "The gate stays closed until we get the dog. He's dangerous."

Jerry let out his breath, then tried again. "The wreck is blocking the highway, man," he lied. "I gotta get there."

The sergeant shrugged, then turned to two uniformed men outside the gate. "Wilson! Andrews! Cover this gate while I open it! We're letting Jerry through."

Jerry put the truck in gear and drove quickly through the open gate. As he drove onto the street, he watched in his rearview mirror as the sergeant slammed the gate closed behind him. He reached out and touched Prince on the head. "That was close!" he told the big dog. Prince licked his hand.

Fifteen minutes later, the big man pulled to the side of the highway, just a mile or two south of town. He walked around to the other side of the truck, climbed up on the running board and opened the door. "Let's have a look at that wound," he said. "I can't do much, but maybe I can stop the bleeding some." He tore the sleeve of his shirt to make a bandage.

Prince didn't let out a whimper as the man gently wrapped the makeshift bandage around his hip, looping the cloth around his leg and over his back to keep it from slipping. Jerry had used most of his shirt by the time he was finished. When the bandage was in place, the big man gritted his teeth as he gently but firmly pulled the cloth tighter. "Sorry if it's hurting you, old friend," he whispered.

When the last knot was tied he pressed gently on the bandage, a big grin of satisfaction on his face. "I think we got the bleedin' stopped," he told Prince. "It's the best I can do." He walked around to his side of the truck, climbed into the cab, and pulled the truck back onto the highway.

Half an hour later he stopped the big tow truck again. "Sorry, old friend," he told Prince, "but this is as far as I can take you. At least you're outta the city. I got a gravel truck to pick up half a mile from here, and it just wouldn't do for anyone to see you in mah truck."

With a grunt, he picked up the big dog and carried him to the shade of a bridge spanning a small stream at the edge of the woods. He gently placed the Labrador in the tall grass a few yards from the water's edge. "Good luck," he told Prince softly. "I wish there was something more I could do for you." He suddenly snapped his fingers and hurried back to his truck.

When Jerry returned he unwrapped a small package and placed it on the grass beside the big dog. Prince feebly licked the big man's hand, and then the man was gone. The dog sniffed at the package his kindhearted rescuer had left. It contained two bologna sandwiches.

Chapter 13
ANGEL OF MERCY

The injured Prince lay beneath the bridge for three days, slowing regaining his strength. The bleeding had entirely stopped, and the wound was beginning to heal. But a fever raged through his body, and he drank from the stream repeatedly.

Jerry's sandwiches had disappeared the first day, but the big dog was too weak to hunt small game as before, and now hunger began to gnaw at his belly. It was the need for food that finally drove him from his resting-place beneath the bridge. He was still weak and unsteady on his feet, but he began to limp slowly southward. Fortunately, the ride in Jerry's truck had carried him nearly forty miles closer to his ultimate goal.

A rabbit dashed across his path that first afternoon, but he was too weak even to give chase. Unknown to him, the lead bullet was still in his hip, and infection was beginning to set in.

Prince found a paper bag that a careless motorist had tossed from a car, and he tore into it eagerly. The bag contained two hamburgers and a number of French fries. The food was nearly two days old, but the big dog did not care. He wolfed it down, then continued on his way. When the highway turned southwest, he left it and continued to travel southward.

For two days he struggled onward. His strength was rapidly diminishing. The fever raged furiously. The infection from the policeman's bullet was slowly killing him. Finally, on the evening of the second day he collapsed in the ditch beside the gravel road he was traveling. Just a few yards away was a small, white house. The magnificent Labrador was more dead than alive.

* * *

Daisy O'Dell had lived beside the road leading to Paulina Lake for more than forty years. She had come to Deschutes County as the young bride of Jim O'Dell, and together they had reared four children in the little white house. The children were grown and married, and Jim had passed away nearly five years ago. Daisy now lived alone.

She still kept one cow, and she had an elderly cat for company. Her needs were simple, and the monthly pension check usually met expenses.

Daisy sat on the front porch one evening, watching the fireflies come out for their evening dance. Her hands, as usual, were busily quilting. The cat, Muffin, sauntered up on the porch and curled up at her feet.

Daisy hurried into the house for a saucer of milk.

She returned a moment later, set the milk in front of the cat now stretched out on the porch railing, then sat down and resumed her quilting. Suddenly she paused, needle poised, listening intently. "These old ears must be playing tricks on me," she told herself, and thrust the needle into the bright material again.

A moment later, she again heard a low moan. "Sounds like someone needs help," the old woman said worriedly, laying the quilting project to one side. She walked to the front gate, glanced up and down the road, but saw nothing.

Just then another moan issued from the edge of the road. Daisy leaned over the gate, then caught her breath in surprise. A large, dark form was lying in the ditch, right beside her gate! With trembling hands, she hurriedly unlatched the gate and knelt beside the figure.

"Oh, my!" she breathed, stroking the head of the motionless Prince. "You're just about gone, poor thing!" She thought quickly. If the big dog were to be saved, there was no time to lose. She had to have help. With a look of determination in her eye, she walked as briskly as she could down the gravel road.

The neighbor turned on the porch light when she

knocked. "Mrs. O'Dell! What is it?" he asked when he saw her troubled face.

"Hank, I need your help, and I need it quickly!" the old woman blurted. "Have Donna call Doc Williams, and have him come up to my place right away. Tell him it's an emergency!"

"Something wrong with your cow?" Hank questioned.

"No," the old woman answered, "I've got a big dog up at my place, and I think he's dying. Can you and Bobby come and help me with him?"

"We'll take the truck," the man answered.

Two minutes later Daisy O'Dell was bouncing along the rutted road in the cab of the neighbor's pickup, her thin figure sandwiched in between the broad-shouldered farmer and his tall teenage son. The veterinarian had already been called. "I came down as soon as I found him," she said worriedly. "I must have done the half-mile to your place in less than ten minutes. I sure hope Doc can pull him through. He don't look good at all."

The three knelt beside the road, studying the lifeless dog. "Let's get him in the house quickly," Daisy suggested. "I do hope Doc gets here soon." Hank and his son rolled Prince onto an old horse blanket, then carried the heavy, silent form of the big dog into the house. "Just set him here in front of the window," Daisy instructed.

When the big dog was situated on the rug in the front room, Daisy brought a bowl of water and tried to get him to drink. But he still didn't stir or open his eyes. His sides heaved with the effort of breathing. The old woman's eyes grew moist as she gently stroked his head, watching his tortured struggle for life. Finally, headlights flashed across the wall of the room as a car pulled into the driveway, and she hurried to the door to meet the vet.

Doc Williams was as much a part of Deschutes County as the sunset. He had grown up in the area, gone to college in California, then returned to the little town of La Pine to practice veterinary medicine. He had been "the Doc" to the rural people for nearly forty years, always ready to care for their pets and livestock at a moment's notice. Tall and stooped, he was widely known as a skillful veterinarian.

Daisy met him at the car. "Hurry, Doc!" she urged. "I'm afraid the poor critter doesn't have much time!" He followed her quickly into the house.

The old woman knelt on the rug beside the huge dog, watching intently as the skilled man examined the animal. He opened his black bag, withdrew a syringe, and quickly gave an injection. While she watched, he inserted a clear plastic tube into a bottle filled with an IV solution, attached a large needle, then inserted the needle in Prince's neck. His fingers moved swiftly as he taped the needle in place.

He turned to her. "You were right, Daisy," he said. "He didn't have much time. Where'd he come from?"

She shook her head. "I really don't know. I found him in my ditch half an hour ago." She looked at the quiet dog, then back up at the doctor. "Will he make it?"

The vet shook his head. "He doesn't have much of a chance, but I'll do my best. He has a nasty hip wound, and the infection has nearly killed him. I'd say he somehow took a bullet. I can't find an exit wound, so I'm guessing the bullet is still in him. I need to try to take it out."

He looked at Hank. "Can you and Bobby help me get him to the kitchen table?" he asked. "I'll operate right here. There isn't time to get him to my office." The three men carried the dog to the table, while the woman carried the IV bottle for them.

The doctor washed his hands, then began to shave the area around the bullet wound. Daisy left the room when he began to probe for the bullet, and the neighbors slipped out to their truck. Doc Williams worked on alone. When he was finished, he called all three of them back into the kitchen.

"I took out a good-sized slug," he told Daisy, handing her a small bowl with a dark object rattling around in the bottom. "I'd say it's from a forty-five."

He looked at the men. "Let's get him back to the other room, shall we? Daisy, you get the IV for us."

When Prince was settled again on the rug, Hank and his son said good-bye and headed for home. The tall vet hooked a new IV bottle in place, adjusted the amount of flow, then turned to the worried woman.

"His chances aren't good, Daisy. I've done all I can, but he probably won't make it through the night. I'll check on him first thing in the morning. I wish I could have had a chance at him yesterday."

He suddenly looked sad. "It's too bad," he said softly. "He was a beautiful dog."

Chapter 14
"HERO"

Daisy sat up with Prince all night. She tried several times to spoon warm milk down his throat, but the liquid just dribbled onto the rug. She prayed as she watched him, hoping to see him begin to show some signs of life. But he never moved. His deep, tortured breathing troubled her, but at least she knew that he was still alive. Finally, just before sunrise, she fell asleep on the rug beside him.

A knock at the door brought her awake with a start. She was embarrassed to see bright sunlight streaming in the front windows. "I didn't even milk Tina," she scolded herself as she hurried to the door.

She opened the door to find Doc Williams standing on the porch. "How's my patient?" he greeted her cheerfully.

"I don't know, Doc," she answered drowsily. "He ain't ever waked up yet."

He shook his head when he heard that. "That's not a good sign. I was hoping he'd be conscious by now."

She led him into the room, and he knelt on the rug and examined Prince, taking his vital signs and checking his temperature. "It's still not looking good," he told her, as he put the thermometer back in his case. "His fever's as high as ever, which means the infection's still strong. That's not good."

He took a new IV bottle from the case. "The IV is giving him the fluids which he so badly needs right now," he told her. "And I'm giving him a powerful antibiotic, the best we have. There's not much else we can do." He stood up. "Only time will tell. At least he made it through the night."

He handed her a second bottle. "I'll step up the flow on the IV, and I'll show you how to change the bottles for him. We're doing all we can do for him. He may just be too far gone."

Shortly after noon, a late-model pickup pulled into the driveway, and a stocky, bearded figure knocked twice, then opened the door. "Ma?" the man called as he walked in. "Where are you?" He stopped at the sight of the big dog on the rug, and stood staring.

Daisy walked into the room. "Hello, Buck," she said, smiling. "How are the children? How's Alisha?"

The man turned to her. "Ma, where did this animal come from?"

She smiled at the astonished look on his face. "He dropped in last night," she replied. "I found him in the ditch. He's been shot. Doc and I are trying to save him."

Buck O'Dell was Daisy's eldest son. A carpenter like his father had been, he and his wife, Alisha, lived in La Pine, less than ten miles away. They had two daughters. Buck always stopped every other day to check on his mother.

He frowned at the big dog. "You know you can't keep him, Ma."

"And why not?" she snapped. "I'm a grown woman! I'll make my own decisions, thank you!"

Buck held up his hands. "Sorry!" he blurted. "I didn't mean it that way, but you know as well as I do that you can't afford to feed an animal of this size. He'd eat you out of house and home in no time!"

She just shrugged. "We're not even sure he's going to make it," she replied. "Doc says he's in a bad way."

Buck turned to face her. "How much have you spent on the vet so far?"

She looked defensive. "Seventy-five dollars. But Doc says that's all he's going to charge me."

"Seventy-five dollars!" Buck echoed. "Ma, that's two weeks' groceries for you! You can't afford this animal!"

Daisy shrugged again. "I'm gonna save him if I can. And if he makes it, I'm gonna keep him. I've been mighty lonely since your pa died. Maybe this big critter could sort of keep me company."

"You have Muffin," the man argued.

The old woman snorted. "You mean, Muffin has me," she retorted. "I care for that cat the best I know how, but does she ever return any favors? Not that one! She's about as affectionate as a brick wall!

"What I need is a dog. You've said so yourself! 'Ma, you ought to get yourself a dog for protection, living out alone like you do. You're sixty-seven years old. Your closest neighbor is half a mile away!'" she quoted him. "Remember saying that?"

Buck looked disgusted. "Don't use my own words against me, Ma," he complained. "Perhaps you do need a dog. But this thing is a horse! Do you have any idea how much a dog his size will eat in a week?"

The old woman waved her hand impatiently. "Son," she said, "I appreciate your concern and all that. But I've already decided. If the dog makes it, I'm keeping him! Say hello to Alisha for me."

That evening Prince woke up. He licked Daisy's hand feebly as she lifted his head and tried to get him to drink some warm milk, then he drifted back to sleep. The old woman was encouraged. Maybe there was hope after all.

The next morning when Doc Williams stopped by, he found the big dog curled up on a rug in the kitchen. The tall vet turned to Daisy in surprise. "Who carried him in here?"

"He carried hisself!" the old woman said, smiling. "I think he's gonna be all right. I got him to drink a little milk last night."

The man nodded, pleased. "That's a good sign. He may pull through yet." He knelt and checked the animal's vital signs. Prince woke up and began slowly licking the vet's gnarled hand.

"His fever's dropped considerably," he told the woman. "Not back to normal yet, but there's been a great deal of improvement. It's still too early to tell, but right now I'd say that his chances are better than fifty-fifty."

He gave Prince another injection, then unhooked the IV tube. Taking a bottle of milky-white liquid from his satchel, he handed it to Daisy. "Try to give him two tablespoons of this four times a day," he instructed. "Mix it in with some milk or some of his food. He'll probably be thirsty; make sure that he has plenty of water at all times.

"I'll check in with you in a couple of days."

Buck stopped in the next afternoon with his two daughters, ten-year-old Lisa and twelve-year-old Emily. Daisy greeted them at the door, with Prince standing quietly beside her.

"Oh, Daddy, he's huge!" Lisa exclaimed, kneeling in front of Prince to throw her arms around his neck. "Can we take him home today?"

Buck looked embarrassed as he turned to Daisy. "Ma," he began, "Alisha had a good idea regarding this big pet of yours. Why not let us take him? That way you'd know that he has a good home, and I'd bring him to see you when I come by."

"And he'd be your dog instead of mine! No, Buck, he stays here with me. I've decided to name him Hero." Daisy's flareup subsided. "Don't you think he looks a lot better?"

The man nodded, disappointed at his mother's insistence on keeping the dog. "He does look better, Ma," he agreed. "But when you decide that you can't afford him anymore, let us know."

"Don't hold your breath!" she shot back.

The girls fussed over Prince for nearly an hour, petting him and brushing out his coat with an old currycomb that their grandmother handed them. Lisa begged to be allowed to take him for a walk.

"Not just yet," Daisy answered. "He's not up to it yet. In a few days, he'll be strong enough, and then you can take him."

It wasn't long before the magnificent Labrador

recovered. Even Doc Williams was amazed at how quickly he bounced back to complete health. To Daisy, he was the sunshine in her day. She took him for long walks on his new leash, and at home he followed her about the house. Just as Buck had feared, the massive dog did consume huge amounts of food, but Daisy had already decided he was worth it.

Every few days Buck or Alisha would bring up the subject of letting them keep the big dog for her, but she always turned them down. Hero would stay with her. If there ever was any doubt in anyone's mind that she would keep the dog, it was erased late one stormy night.

Chapter 15
THE BURGLAR

Alisha stopped by the farm one rainy afternoon. She was a pretty woman, tall and slender. Her dark hair hung in loose curls past her shoulders. Daisy watched from the window as Alisha got out of the truck, and was surprised to see a small black poodle on a leash following her.

She met Alisha at the door. "Come in, Alisha. It's good to see you, dear. You haven't been here in a week. Where did you get that little snip of a dog?"

Prince and the poodle sniffed noses as the younger woman handed Daisy the leash. "He's for you. Buck and I picked him out yesterday."

Daisy frowned, puzzled. "But I already have a dog. Hero would be mighty upset with me if I got a second one."

Alisha sat down in the front room. "Mom, listen," she said. "Buck and I know that you've been lonely since Dad died, and you should have a dog. But Hero is going to be too much for you. We got Pierre, here, hoping that you'd allow us to take Hero for you. Pierre would be good company, and Hero would have a good home with us. And like Buck promised, we'd bring him by to see you."

Daisy sighed deeply. "Alisha, dear," she said, "I've told Buck a hundred times already—Hero stays here! He's my dog, and he stays with me. And that's final. But thanks for the offer. You and Buck keep Pierre."

That evening a storm set in with a fury. Lightning slashed viciously across the darkening skies, and heavy thunder echoed back and forth across the valley. The rain fell in torrents, and the wind howled and moaned like a creature in pain. Daisy and Hero were soaked as they dashed across to the little barn for the evening milking.

After supper Daisy went out on the porch to quilt and watch the storm, but the wind gusted and blew the rain in on the porch. Finally she and the big dog retreated to the comfort of the front room. The rain was still pelting the roof of the little house as the old woman retired early.

Several hours later Daisy sat up in bed with a start, awakened by a loud noise. Crash! There it was again! And then another crash. Clutching her housecoat about her, she hurried from the bedroom. This storm was going to tear the house down.

She turned on the front room light, then cried out in fear. A tall man was standing in the room, blinking in the sudden brightness of the light! Shards of broken glass littered the floor beneath the broken window he had climbed through.

Daisy threw her hands to her mouth in shock, then took a bold step forward. "What are you doing in my house?" she demanded.

The man leaped forward and caught one thin wrist in a bone-crushing grip. His other hand whipped out a long, wicked-looking knife. "Old woman," he snarled, "don't make a sound! If you don't make trouble, you won't get hurt!"

Daisy was furious. "Get out of my house!" she demanded. "When I call the sheriff, you'll wish you had never set foot in this place!"

"Go ahead and call!" the burglar sneered. "You ain't got no phone!" He jerked her closer to him and held the knife to her throat. Suddenly Daisy felt a stab of fear. This man wouldn't even hesitate to kill her! "Get back in the bedroom and close the door," he told her, shoving her backward. "If you open it so much as a crack, I'll kill you!" The old woman had no doubt that he meant it.

At that instant Hero pushed open the door and entered the room with a vicious growl. He had been sleeping in the kitchen and had awakened at the sound of angry voices. The tall thug slashed desperately with the knife as the Labrador leaped for his throat.

The force of the big dog's attack knocked the knife from the man's grasp and sent it skittering across the hardwood floor. The burglar fell heavily to the floor with the snarling, snapping dog on top of him. The man was terrified. "Get him off me!" he screamed.

He rolled free of the dog, who immediately pounced on him again. Blood spurted from a deep gash in the man's calf, and his blood-soaked shirt gave a hint of other injuries. The man held his arms up for protection, kicking and struggling. "Call him off!" he begged. "He's killing me!"

Daisy ran forward. "Hero!" she shouted. "Hero! Down, boy!"

Prince hesitated, and the man scrambled to his feet and made a dash for the door. The big dog looked at his mistress, then lunged at the man again. The tall burglar got the door opened just in time and fled the house with Prince hard on his heels.

Daisy went to the front door and looked out. A brilliant white bolt of lightning lit the sky just then, and she could see the silhouette of the man running desperately down the road, the angry dog just a step behind him.

An old red car was parked on the road, its engine

idling. The old woman went out to the car and turned off the ignition, removed the key, and dropped it in the pocket of her housecoat. With a determined smile on her wrinkled face, she then let the air out of all four tires.

Prince appeared on the porch a few minutes later. Taking an umbrella from the closet, Daisy and the big dog set off through the rain to use Hank's phone.

The sheriff's car left just after the tow truck had taken the burglar's car away. "I don't think he'll be back tonight, Miss Daisy," the lawman had chuckled. "From what you told us, I think we'll start looking for him by checking the local hospitals!"

Buck stopped by the next morning. "They caught him!" were his first words to his mother as she let him in. "He was bleeding pretty badly, and he checked into Good Samaritan Hospital. Hero really tore him up!"

He suddenly looked grave. "Ma, you're lucky you had the dog," he said. "Sheriff Adams called and told me about the arrest. That guy had a record a mile long. He had killed a man during an armed robbery and had been serving a life sentence. He escaped from San Quentin this spring."

Daisy looked up at him. "Still going to try to talk

me into giving Hero to you? Pierre wouldn't have been much help last night!"

Buck shook his head, grinning. "We'll just help you pay for his keep, if you need us to."

The old woman shook her head. "You just take care of that poodle that you tried to pawn off on me," she said, laughing. "Hero and I can take care of ourselves."

"I do wish you'd get a phone put in though, Ma."

Daisy snorted. "If I had one of those contraptions," she replied, "I'd never get a moment's work done around here. No, thanks. On the two or three occasions each year that I need to use the phone, I'll just walk down to Hank's place. And if there's ever any more trouble, I still have Hero."

Buck frowned. "Well, I'm not gonna try to talk you into it. But I am glad you have the dog."

Chapter 16
DAISY'S DECISION

Summer was over. Lisa and Emily had started back to school. Buck and Alisha were busier than usual, and they did not stop by to see Daisy as frequently as they had in the past. The old woman was grateful for Prince's company.

"You always have time for me, don't you, Hero?" she crooned to him on one of their long walks. "Sometimes it seems like no one has time for an old woman, but you always do." They walked on in silence, the old woman thankful for the friendship of the big Labrador.

"I really don't know how I ever made it without you," she told the dog a few minutes later. "Ever since Jim died, I have been so lonely. Buck and Alisha have been very good to me, but they have their own lives and family. I'm glad I have you. You've done wonders for me, Hero."

Saturday morning Buck dropped off Emily and Lisa at Daisy's to spend the day. The girls took Prince for a walk while their grandmother did her cleaning. Lisa proudly held the leash as they walked along.

"He's so big, it's almost scary," the dark-haired girl

commented to her older sister as they strolled along. "If he decides to go somewhere, I guess I had better want to go there too, 'cause I sure can't stop him!"

Her older sister laughed. "I know," she agreed. "It would be like trying to stop a bulldozer with your bare hands." She watched the massive dog for a minute, then remarked, "You know, though, I think he'd just stop if you told him to. He's so gentle." The girls both agreed that he was the best dog they had ever seen.

Emily took her turn holding the leash as they sauntered back down the gravel road. Hank passed in his pickup, waving to the girls as they stepped from the roadway to avoid the cloud of dust raised by his truck.

When they returned to the house, Daisy had lemonade and jelly tarts waiting. She even gave a tart to Prince, and the girls giggled as they watched him eat it. When they had finished the snack, their grandmother called them into the front room.

"Hero and I want to demonstrate a trick or two for you," she said. The girls sat side by side on the old, faded sofa.

Daisy held a rolled-up newspaper with a rubber band around it. "Hero, fetch!" she called, tossing the paper across the narrow room. The big dog bounded after the paper, then brought it back in his mouth to the old woman.

The girls were surprised when their grandmother refused to take it. "I don't want it, Hero," she told the dog. "Take it to Emily." To their surprise, he walked over and laid the paper in the older girl's lap.

"How did he know?" they both chorused, but the old woman just laughed. "That's his secret," she said, smiling. "I promised him I wouldn't tell."

"Emily, toss it for him, would you, Sweetheart?" she requested. The girl tossed the paper, but Daisy called out, "Hero, wait!" The big dog sat patiently, tail wagging, his eyes on Daisy. "Tell him to bring it," she whispered to the girls.

"Fetch it, Hero!" Lisa and Emily both called. "Go get it, boy! Fetch!" But the big dog still sat motionless.

Finally Daisy spoke up. "It's okay, Hero. Fetch!" Prince bounded across the room and brought the paper back to the old lady.

But as before, she refused it. "I don't want it, Hero," she told him. "Take it to Lisa." To the delight of both her granddaughters, the dog knew again which girl to take it to.

The woman and the dog repeated the performance a number of times. Each time the command was different. "Take it to the girl in the blue dress." Again, the big dog got it right. "Take it to the girl who is youngest." And Prince did. "Take it to the girl on the left. Take it to the girl who has her legs crossed." And every time, Prince got it right.

"How does he know that, Grandma?" Lisa pleaded. "Please tell us!"

But Daisy just smiled and replied, "You wouldn't have me break a promise to Hero, would you? Ask him! He can tell you if he wishes."

Lisa called the Labrador over to her and asked, "How did you do it, Hero? How did you know who to take it to?" But of course, the big dog wasn't telling.

"Now watch this, girls," Daisy said. "This is Hero's favorite trick." When she called, "Battle stations!" Prince marched grandly to the center of the room and stood proudly, almost as if he were standing guard at some army post. Daisy walked forward and called, "Sit up, Hero." The big dog sat up on his haunches, his forelegs held up against his chest. The girls clapped in delight.

"Watch this," their grandmother whispered. She walked forward and pointed her finger at Prince like a gun, then said, "Bang!" With a yelp, the gigantic dog fell over on the floor and lay still. The girls were amazed. Finally Daisy said, "You're okay, Hero. Get up." The dog promptly sprang to his feet and trotted over to the woman to be petted and praised.

The girls were in awe. "He is the smartest dog we've ever seen, Granny!" Lisa exclaimed. "Can we make him do that?"

As Buck drove them home later that day, both girls chattered excitedly about the tricks that Prince had performed. "You should have seen him, Daddy!" Lisa bubbled. "He's the smartest dog I ever saw!"

On Monday Daisy called Doc Williams from Hank's place. "Can you stop by sometime soon?" she asked. "No emergency. I just want to ask you something about Hero. Just stop in when it's convenient for you. But if you can, let yourself in the north gate, and come to the back door without Hero seeing you."

Doc stopped by that evening. "I was just coming back from doing some testing on MacIntyre's cattle," he told Daisy at the back door. "What's on your mind?"

"It's Hero," the old woman told him soberly. "He's been acting strange for the last couple of weeks. Maybe it's nothing, but I wanted to see what you think. Please come in."

She led the veterinarian to the window of the front room and drew back the faded yellow lace curtains. "Watch him for a minute. Tell me what you think."

Doc Williams watched Prince for a moment or two. The big dog was pacing along the fence at the edge of the yard, whining and looking off into the distance. He leaped up with his front paws on the top of the fence, barked twice, then resumed his restless pacing.

"How long has he been doing this?" the man asked.

"About two weeks, I guess," the worried woman answered. "What's wrong with him? As you can see, he's worn a path along the entire south side of the yard, just inside the fence. What's ailin' him?"

Doc looked thoughtful. "He acts like he wants to get out pretty bad, doesn't he? Maybe he wants to get at another dog."

The old woman shook her head. "Ain't no dogs in that direction for over two miles."

The tall vet hesitated, then answered slowly, "Daisy, I hate to tell you this, but I think Hero wants to leave. He has something or someone calling him away from you."

Daisy was puzzled. "Why would he want to leave me? I've been good to him."

The man nodded. "There's no denying that. But a

Labrador is a very loyal dog. Once he develops a loyalty to one master, he'll maintain that loyalty for the rest of his life.

"You found Hero when he was dying, and you saved his life. He's developed a certain loyalty to you as a result. In fact, it's only that loyalty that is keeping him here right now. He could jump that fence of yours in an instant, if he really wanted to. It's loyalty to you that keeps him from doing so. But one day the stronger loyalty will take him from you."

"But I love him!" the woman protested. "I couldn't make it through the day without him! And he loves me."

The vet nodded. "I'm sure that feeling is mutual," he replied. "You met a real need for the dog, and he has met a need in your life. But again, I really believe his loyalty to you is secondary. That's only a guess, but I really believe that's why he's been acting that way."

"I can keep him in the house," Daisy replied.

"As a prisoner?" the vet questioned. "Daisy, would you really want that for him?"

"Well," she answered, "just till he gets over it and develops a lasting loyalty to me."

The man shook his head. "I don't think that's going to happen. How long has he been with you?"

Daisy cocked her head to one side, thinking. "Almost two months now."

Doc Williams nodded. "The other loyalty is never going to diminish. In fact, now that he's well, his restlessness is probably going to grow stronger."

Daisy was troubled. She sat silently for several minutes. The doctor stood by the window watching the big Labrador. Finally she looked up at him. "What do you think I need to do?" she reluctantly asked.

"Give him his freedom," the man said gently. "Tell him it's okay to find his other master, if that is what's troubling him. There's a chance that I'm wrong and he won't leave. But I really don't think he'll ever be completely happy, and neither will you, if you try to keep him here."

He smiled sadly at the tears in her eyes. "I'm sorry, Daisy, if I've upset you. But I really think that is what's ailing your dog. Now it's up to you."

He let himself out the back door. Prince never heard him as he left. But the kind doctor noticed as he drove by the house that the big dog was still pacing along the fence on the south side of the yard.

For the next two days Daisy tried to forget the old doctor's words. But every time she looked at Prince, a huge lump rose in her throat. Finally she determined that setting him free was the only right thing to do. But she never had the chance to carry out her decision.

That afternoon, two young boys selling greeting cards timidly approached the house. When they opened the front gate, the big Labrador was out and running down the road. Daisy saw what was happening and ran from the house calling, "Hero! Hero! Come back, Hero!" But the big dog was gone.

The two boys were apologetic. "We didn't mean to let him out, ma'am," the taller of the two told her earnestly. "Honest we didn't! We tried to catch him, but he was too fast!"

Daisy nodded, trying to blink back the tears. "It's all right, Son," she told the boy softly. "Maybe it was for the best anyway. Now don't fret about it."

When the boys were gone, the old woman walked down to Hank's place. She stopped in front of the house to wipe her eyes and blow her nose. Then she knocked on the door and asked to use the phone.

"Buck," she said in a tiny voice, "does the offer of the poodle still stand? I think I'm gonna be lonely tonight, and I could use his company. I'll tell you about it when you get here." Her chin was quivering as she hung up the phone.

Chapter 17
THE DOG POUND

The afternoon sun beat down fiercely as Prince journeyed down the dusty gravel road. The big dog was again traveling south, and he assumed a steady, mile-consuming pace. He was going home.

Suddenly a horn blared beside him. He leaped to the side of the road as a station wagon roared past, covering him with a cloud of dust. Wary now, he headed for the bushes at the side of road whenever he heard a vehicle approaching. By midafternoon he was hot, tired and dusty. A little creek flowed quietly under a narrow wooden bridge, and he was glad to stop and refresh himself, drinking greedily, then rolling and splashing in the cool water.

That evening he was passing through a small village when a heavyset, friendly-looking man with a heavy black mustache called to him. "Hey, boy!" the man whistled. "Come here, boy!" Prince stopped in the road and looked him over warily.

"Whatsa matter?" the man asked. "You don't trust me?" The man squatted beside the back door of his restaurant, patting his thick thigh vigorously. "Come here, boy!" he called softly. "I won't hurt you."

Slowly, cautiously, Prince went to him. As the man slowly held out one hand to him, Prince sniffed it uneasily. When the man stood up, the big dog jumped, then quickly retreated a few feet.

"It's all right, boy!" the man said quietly. "Stay here. Stay! I have something for you."

He disappeared inside his shop, then reappeared almost instantly with a large dish. "Here," he said to Prince. "You look hungry. No use letting this go to waste." He set the dish on the sidewalk, then backed off a few feet.

Prince cautiously approached the dish, then began to gulp the generous offering of spicy meat. He was hungry, and the food quickly disappeared.

A large woman came to the door. "Tony!" she scolded. "Are you feeding another animal? No wonder we can't make any money! You give all our profits away!"

The heavy man shrugged. "Maria, my love," he said with a grin, "it is just leftovers! The dog was hungry. Tomorrow I make more."

"Tomorrow we buy more," Maria corrected him. "The butcher does not give the meat to you. This restaurant will never make any money if you insist on feeding every stray dog and cat that wanders through. How many tacos and enchiladas would that have made?"

"But he is not just a stray," Tony argued. "Look at him! Such a magnificent animal!"

"I'm sure that he ate a magnificent amount of ground beef," Maria returned.

Prince finished his meal and sat back on the sidewalk, licking his chops. The friendly man picked up the empty dish. "Thanks for stopping by," he told Prince. "Come again sometime."

The big dog walked over to the man and gravely held out his right paw. Tony shook the paw and laughed. "It's been a pleasure doing business with you."

For the next several days Prince was on his own. He was traveling through sparsely populated territory, but he was now an accomplished hunter. Rabbits were in abundance, and they provided the bulk of his meals. Occasionally he met up with some kindhearted person like the generous Tony, and then he ate especially well.

Whenever he found a road leading south, he would take it, as it usually afforded him the easiest way of traveling. But much of the time he was traveling in the wild, always heading due south, occasionally detouring around lakes and rivers.

Late one evening, unknown to him, he crossed the state line into Nevada. Oregon was finally left behind. For two days he journeyed across the northwestern tip of the state. On the morning of the third day he crossed another state line. Finally he was back in his home state of California. But there were still many miles ahead.

That morning while Prince was making his way up a hill through the tall grasses that had taken over a deserted farm, a strange, buzzing noise suddenly caught his attention. He stopped, trying to pinpoint the source of the sound. His sensitive nose picked up a strange, wild scent.

As he stepped forward, a brown flash struck at him. He quickly leaped to one side. The five-foot diamondback rattlesnake coiled again for another strike, but the big dog retreated hurriedly. Instinct told him that this was no creature to be messed with.

That afternoon he reached the town of Ravendale. Hungry and tired, he caught the scent of food as he trotted down a busy sidewalk. He followed his nose to a back alley. Behind a restaurant he found a garbage can nearly filled with table scraps left over by the diners that day. As he tipped over the can, a deep-throated snarl caught his attention.

He turned just as a Doberman pinscher and two large mongrels entered the enclosure behind the restaurant. Fangs bared, the Doberman immediately sprang for Prince's throat, while the mongrels warily circled him.

Prince was hopelessly outnumbered, but he fought gamely. As the Doberman struck, the Labrador twisted sideways, slashing out at his attacker. His teeth found the ear of the other dog, tearing a gash in it. The Doberman yelped, then lunged in again. As he did, the two mongrels also attacked.

As they came, Prince charged straight at them, snapping at one of the mongrels as he shot past. He dashed for the back stoop of the restaurant, then whirled about to face his attackers. His hindquarters were now protected from an assault from the rear.

The three dogs closed in on him again. When they were within striking distance, Prince suddenly lunged forward. The Labrador's jaws found the fore-leg of the other dog, and there was a snapping sound as he bit down. The mongrel gave a yelp of pain, then dashed away as fast as he could go on three legs. Now there were only two dogs fighting against Prince.

Prince sprang at the remaining mongrel, and the

Doberman leaped at him, biting viciously. His teeth found their mark, and the big Labrador gave a yelp of pain as his cheek was gashed open.

He twisted away from the other dogs and circled around to put himself in position for their next attack. As he did, a large net came swooshing over him, and a man in a khaki uniform jerked him off his feet. He dragged Prince across the pavement to the rear of a truck. The other dogs fled.

"Help me, Pete," the dogcatcher called to his companion in the truck. "This one's heavy!" The other man climbed out of the cab, and together the two men lifted Prince through a small door in the back of the truck. The net was removed, and the dog found himself trapped with three other captives in a steel cage.

A short while later the two men backed the truck in behind a building and began to unload the dogs into cages. "Here's a good-looking one," Pete said as he and his partner put Prince into a cage. "He doesn't look like your usual stray. Wonder how he got here."

"We'll never know," Al said, locking the gate of the enclosure. "I hope somebody picks him up before his time's up, though. It'd be a shame to have to destroy an animal like him." Prince was now a captive in the city pound.

Three days later, a young couple came into the pound. They wandered through the building, stopping occasionally to examine one of the dogs. When they came to Prince, the man shook his head firmly and started to walk on by, but the woman pulled him back.

"Oh, look, Roy," she said, gazing wonderingly at the huge Labrador. "Look at the size of him!"

Roy nodded. "He probably weighs as much as I do, and eats three times as much," he answered. "Don't get any ideas about taking him home, Lana. We could never afford to feed a creature his size!"

"I was just looking at him," Lana answered. "He sure is a nice-looking dog. Can you imagine what the neighbors would say if I walked him down our street?"

"Forget it!" the man answered. "I'm gonna be lucky just to afford to support a wife, let alone a monster like him! Come on, let's look at the other dogs."

At that moment, Prince stuck his right paw out through the mesh of the cage. Lana laughed delightedly and shook it. "Look, Roy, he's friendly!"

Roy laughed and put an arm around his young wife's shoulder. "Come on, Honey. Let's look at the other dogs in here."

"Oh, look, Roy," the woman cried. "He's hurt!"

Her husband nodded. "Looks like he's been in a

fight. I'd sure hate to see the other dog, if he could go up against a brute this size!"

The couple wandered through the pound, lingering in front of one cage, then another. Finally Al came into the kennel area and approached them. "Made up your mind yet?" he asked pleasantly.

"How much is it to get a dog?" Roy asked him.

"Thirty dollars, sir," the dogcatcher replied. "Twenty dollars for the shots and ten for the license."

"Are all the dogs the same price, no matter what size they are?" Lana asked.

The man nodded. "They're all the same price, ma'am," he answered. "You're not really buying the dog. You're just paying for the shots and license."

"What happens to the dogs that nobody wants?" Lana asked.

Al paused. "We hold them for three weeks, ma'am. At the end of that time, an unclaimed dog is put to sleep."

Lana turned to Roy. "Let's get the big one, Sweetheart. Please? If no one else takes him, they'll destroy him!"

Roy looked troubled. He glanced at Al for support, then turned back to Lana. "We can't afford to get him, Honey! He'd eat us out of house and home!"

Al grinned. "Newlyweds?"

Lana nodded proudly. "We just got married last week!"

The dogcatcher smiled. "Congratulations! I'll leave you two alone to talk it over." He glanced at Roy. "Good luck!"

Ten minutes later the young couple left the pound with their new dog, a huge Labrador, on a leash. They squeezed the big animal into the back seat of their Nissan, then happily started for home. Lana was all smiles.

* * *

Mr. Patterson found his wife busily shredding cheese for a casserole when he came in from work. He gave her a quick kiss, then tossed the day's mail on the kitchen table. "How'd your day go?"

She smiled at him and shrugged casually. "Okay, I guess. And yours?"

The tall professor grinned. "Fantastic! I've got some really sharp students this quarter. It's going to be a good year!" He stepped to the door of the kitchen and glanced down the hall. "Where are the kids?"

"In the backyard," his wife answered. She glanced up from the grater. "I sure wish Christina could get over this thing about losing Prince! She's still carrying on about him, wondering when he's gonna come home. I tried to talk to her today, but it just doesn't seem to do any good."

He nodded. "Maybe I can get a chance to talk with her later." He swung across the kitchen, taking long strides with the crutches.

"Kenneth."

He spun around on the crutches to face her.

"Do you know what she's basing her hopes on?" Mrs. Patterson asked. "John 14:14."

"'If ye shall ask any thing in my name, I will do it,'" he quoted.

She nodded. "That's the one." She bit her lip thoughtfully. "Oh, Kenneth, do you think there's even the slightest chance? Prince has been gone so long, but Christina's faith hasn't wavered one bit. She still insists that the Lord is going to bring him back to her."

He sighed. "I hope it doesn't crush her if her prayer isn't answered the way she expects. A thing like this could damage a child's faith."

"Do you think…" She stopped, frowned, then continued. "What if God does answer her prayer and bring Prince back? Just to honor Christina's faith, I mean."

He smiled sadly. "I wish it were that simple. And I wish I still had the faith that Christina does. I'll be out in the backyard with the kids for a few minutes."

When he returned to the kitchen, his wife was sitting at the table with a letter in her hand. Her face was pale. She appeared to be in a state of shock. Kenneth walked over and put a hand on her shoulder. "Honey, what's wrong?"

She looked up at him. "It's a letter from Mom. I...I can't believe what I just read. Listen to this."

The back door opened just then, and David and Christina burst into the room. "Mom!" Christina began. "David said that..." She stopped abruptly, seeing the look on her mother's face.

She and her brother stood quietly, unnoticed, as Mrs. Patterson began to read in a trembling voice:

> I've been rather lonely lately, but for the past several weeks I've had a rather unusual pet to keep me company. He was a huge dog, a Labrador. I found him in the ditch in front of my place, nearly dead from a gunshot wound that had become infected. Doc Williams and I were able to save his life.

The dog, which I named Hero, stayed with me for several weeks. You should have seen him. He was gigantic. He reminded me a lot of Prince, that big dog of yours that Christina always talks about. I'd like to see Prince when you come up here for Thanksgiving.

Anyway, I no longer have Hero. He ran away from me just a couple of weeks ago. The last I saw of him, he was heading south along Valley Road like he was going to a fire. I miss him greatly; he was a fine companion.

I just thought you'd be interested, since you have a big dog just like him. Buck got a couple of snapshots of Hero, so I'm enclosing one with this letter. If you please, send it back the next time you write.

Mrs. Patterson stopped reading. With trembling fingers she pulled a photo from the envelope and handed it to her husband. "It's Prince," she said softly.

The professor studied the picture. David and Christina crowded close, clamoring to see it. He handed it to them and remarked, "There's no doubt—it is Prince. But how in the world would he have gotten to your mother's?"

Christina held the photo, dancing around the

kitchen in her excitement. "It is Prince!" she shouted. "He went to Grandma's! Oh, goody! Can we go get him?"

Mrs. Patterson pulled her daughter close. "Prince was at Grandma's, Honey," she explained, "but he's not there anymore. Grandma doesn't know where he is."

"Then he's coming here!" the little girl rejoiced. "God is going to bring him to us! Oh, goody! I just knew He would!"

Mom shook her head sadly. "Grandma's house is over six hundred miles away, Sweetheart," she said gently. "Prince could never find us. He'd never make it that far. He'd have to cross highways and rivers and...well, I'm just afraid he'd never make it that far. I'm sorry, Honey."

Mr. Patterson stared at the letter in his hand. "If only she had written sooner," he said quietly.

Chapter 18
MOUNTAIN LION

Roy and Lana discussed names for their new pet as they drove home. They couldn't settle on one name, so Roy suggested that they give it some thought and decide later. "Perhaps as we get to know him better, a name that fits him will suggest itself," he said. "Now, how do you propose that we pay for his upkeep?"

"I've been thinking about that," Lana answered. "If I'm careful, I can cut a few dollars from what we had planned to spend for groceries. That will help some. I can go back to cleaning Mrs. Austin's house, like I did before we were married. It's only one day a week, and I can make enough to pay for the rest of his food. You don't mind, do you?"

Roy smiled as he said, "Sounds like you've got it all figured out."

Prince lay across the back seat of the little car, panting furiously in the stifling heat. The vehicle was like an oven. Roy stopped the car in the driveway of a small house and opened the door. When he leaned the front seat forward, Prince leaped from the car.

"Stop him!" Lana called. "He'll get away! He doesn't know us yet."

Roy lunged for Prince. It suddenly occurred to the big dog that he was free! He wheeled out of the man's reach, dashed across the yard and leaped over a low fence. Finding himself in an alley, he quickly disappeared down its cluttered passage. Moments later he was at the south edge of town, with no sign of the man or woman pursuing him. He resumed his journey south.

In the next few days Prince made his way through some of the most desolate country he had yet encountered. Steep, barren mountains with their foreboding rocky cliffs and ledges overlooked treacherous canyons and gorges. The going was difficult for the big dog, and water was scarce. His pace slowed through the difficult terrain. Each mile of travel was a hard-won victory.

On several occasions, he came to a precipice or gorge which he simply could not cross, and he had to backtrack and detour around. In one such situation it took him three entire days to find a way around.

Early one morning he found a trickling stream and quenched his burning thirst. The water was cool and refreshing. As he stood in the tiny stream, a rabbit bounded across the stream bank. Prince was upon it in an instant. In three quick leaps the rabbit was his.

He prepared to devour the much-needed meal when a growling snarl caught his ear. He glanced up the steep, rocky incline above him just in time to catch sight of a golden flash of fur as it launched itself upon him.

The region was experiencing a drought, and game was scarce. The cougar had been stalking the furry, bouncing creature, and Prince had interrupted the hunt. The big cat was desperate; now he wanted the rabbit that was pinned beneath the Labrador's paw.

The snarling, spitting, wild animal landed heavily on the dog's back. Prince rolled clear and sprang to one side. His quick reflexes had protected him from injury in the big cat's initial assault, but the angry cougar crouched and sprang again.

This time Prince was ready. Big as he was, he was agile and fast, and he nimbly sidestepped the cougar's charge. Furious, the big cat turned, bounded forward, then leaped high. He landed atop the struggling dog.

Screaming like a banshee, the angry cat lashed out viciously at the dog's side. His sharp, curved claws found their mark, and the dog yelped in pain. He rolled desperately, slashed at the cougar, then bounded clear.

Fortunately, the big cat was attacking in a blind

rage, and his powerful claws did not accomplish the damage of which they were capable. The cougar had torn away a large chunk of hair, and his razor-sharp claws had slashed into the dog's skin, but the wound was not deep.

The big Labrador was no coward, nor was he a fool. Quickly realizing that he was no match for the sharp claws and fangs of the hungry cougar, he turned and dashed desperately down the mountainside. The cougar followed him for a few dozen yards, then returned to the slain rabbit.

Prince paused several hundred yards below in the canyon to lick his wounds. His side was burning where the mountain lion had clawed him, and the blood was matting his fur, but the injury was not life-threatening.

Late that evening he found a tiny trickle of water seeping from the rocky hillside. He satisfied his thirst, but he still had not eaten. He bedded down behind a fallen tree in a dry, rock-strewn wash, still hungry.

The next morning he was able to catch a chuck-walla, a fat, hideous-looking lizard. He eagerly tore into the reptile. The meat had a strong, disagreeable taste, but it was food, and he devoured the entire carcass. It was to be his only meal that day.

Finally, on the third day following the cougar attack, the unfriendly mountains gave way to gently rolling hills, and in just a few more miles the terrain was nearly flat. The worst of the journey was over.

Prince trotted over the crest of a gentle hill and once again entered civilization. A two-lane highway snaked toward the south, and he went down to it.

A shallow, crystal-clear creek tumbled and splashed its way down out of the hills, winding and frolicking over its rocky bed. At the point where the creek reached the highway to flow through a corrugated culvert, the highway department had planted a pleasant rest area for motorists. Three wooden picnic tables sprawled on the lush green carpet of grass that spread down to the very edge of the creek, and a tall stand of poplars shaded the area. The spot was cool and inviting, an oasis from the afternoon heat.

A rust-eaten old van was parked in the gravel at the edge of the rest area, and a small, bearded man was cooking over a small fire built in one of the cast-iron picnic grills beside the tables. He looked up with friendly interest as Prince walked down to the stream for a drink.

"Care to join me for dinner, pooch?" he called in a warm tone to the dog. "I don't know about tomorrow, but I've got more than enough for today."

Four hot dogs were browning on the grill, and the man removed two, whistling in pain as the hot grease burned his fingers. He placed them on a section of newspaper, then set the paper on the ground for Prince. "Hungry?" he asked the dog. "I may not have much, but I'm willing to share what I've got."

Cautiously Prince approached the newspaper, sniffed at the hot dogs, then gulped them down. The man nodded in satisfaction, then pulled the other two hot dogs from the grill. "If you're that hungry," he told Prince, "you might as well eat these too. I can fix myself a peanut butter sandwich."

The big Labrador devoured the last of the hot dogs, then watched as the man walked to his van. He pulled half a loaf of stale bread from the back of the van and began to spread peanut butter with a dirty knife. The man took a bite of the sandwich, then opened a cooler and took out a covered dish.

"Got some stew left," he told the dog, who had walked closer to the van. "It's yours if you want it. Didn't really care much for it myself." He snapped the lid from the dish and placed it on the ground in front of the hungry dog. In no time at all the stew was gone too.

The little man walked over and crouched beside Prince. "What's your name, pooch?" he asked, scratching the dog's ears. "Mine's Denny, Denny O'Brien. You're welcome for the eats."

Fifteen minutes later the old van pulled back onto the highway. Prince was sitting in the front seat, head out the window, enjoying the breeze as Denny drove. An hour later and fifty miles farther south, the van pulled into a little town, and Denny stopped in front of a drugstore to buy a newspaper.

That night they stayed in a tiny, cockroach-infested motel room. Denny cooked over a small electric skillet while Prince gobbled two cans of dog food that the man had bought for him. Denny read the obituaries while his meal cooked.

"Not a bad number of obits for a dinky little town like this," he told Prince. "We'll stay and do business tomorrow."

* * *

Mr. Patterson hurried down the hall toward the staff lounge, swinging his crutches in such long strides that his book satchel banged repeatedly against his back. His intro. to basic programming class had gone well that morning, but he was hungry and looking forward to lunch.

"Patterson!" a voice called. "Wait up!"

He turned to see Dave Andrews, professor of political sciences, rushing toward him. "What's the hurry, Professor?" Andrews said, laughing. "On your way to a fire?"

Mr. Patterson grinned. "Nope. Just hungry. What's on your mind?"

"Did you guys ever find that dog of yours? I heard that your family was pretty upset about losing him."

Mr. Patterson nodded. "Especially my six-year-old. We never did find Prince, but Christina is still praying that God will bring him back to her."

The other professor laughed. "Praying, huh? Patterson, we're entering the twenty-first century! It's time you taught your kids about the real world. Prayer went out with the horse and buggy!"

Mr. Patterson shook his head. "That's where you're wrong, Dave. God still answers prayer—but only for His children."

The other man frowned. "And how does one become one of God's children?" he sneered.

"Simply admit to God that you're a sinner and have broken His laws and commandments," the tall professor replied. "Believe that Jesus, the Son of God, died on the cross to shed His blood for your sins, then rose from the grave the third day. And then, simply by faith ask Jesus to save you. According to the Bible, that's how anyone can become a child of God."

Mr. Patterson expected a sneering reply, but Dave Andrews stood silently studying his face, then said thoughtfully, "You're really serious about this stuff, aren't you? You act as if you really believe it."

"It's real, Dave," Mr. Patterson replied softly. "Jesus Christ died for you. He offers to forgive your sins and give you eternal life if you'll only believe and receive Him by faith."

The other man shook his head. "I'm not ready for this stuff yet. I'm still not convinced." He glanced at his watch. "Hey, gotta run. Have a good lunch."

He started to walk away, then turned back. "Hey, Patterson, if...uh, if God brings that dog back to your little girl, you let me know, huh? Then I just might have time to listen to all this business about faith. Deal?"

Mr. Patterson watched the other professor hurry down the hallway. "Lord," he prayed silently, "is there any way You could bring Prince back? It would sure boost my little girl's faith. And it might even give me a chance to win Dave Andrews. Lord, is it possible?"

Chapter 19
DENNY O'BRIEN

Prince sat patiently at the bottom of the steps as Denny, dressed in a business suit, knocked on the front door of a small farmhouse. The man put on a huge smile as an elderly woman answered the door.

"Good morning, ma'am," Denny said politely as the lady opened the door. "I'm Denny O'Brien with Pacific States Resource Management Specialties. May I speak with Mr. Adams, please?"

The woman dabbed at her eyes with a tissue. "He ain't with us no longer, sir," she answered slowly. "He passed away on Saturday."

A look of sympathy and concern passed across the man's face. "I'm sorry to hear that, ma'am," he said quietly, almost reverently. "Please forgive me for bothering you in your time of sorrow."

He started away from the door, then turned back. "Please excuse me, ma'am," he said gently, "but would you be Mrs. Adams?"

The woman nodded sorrowfully. "George and I was married for 'most thirty years."

"Is your name Martha?" the man asked gently.

The woman's head jerked up as she stared at her

visitor in surprise. "How did you know that?" she asked.

Denny opened a leather-bound folder, produced an embossed document, then handed it to her. "You and your husband are listed as the owners of the mineral rights to a tract of land in Wyoming."

Mrs. Adams frowned. "We never bought land in Wyoming."

Denny shook his head. "This is land belonging to the federal government, ma'am. The government grants mineral and mining rights to private citizens who file the proper paperwork. Two years ago your husband acquired the rights to a Wyoming tract. He registered in both your names, so the rights are yours if he is deceased."

He paused. "I believe I have good news for you, Mrs. Adams. Two months ago the Gibraltar Oil Company filed for a lease to drill on the property to which you hold the rights. This will produce an annual income of several thousand dollars for you. In the event that they do find oil, your royalties could amount to hundreds of thousands of dollars!"

The woman's eyes opened wide in astonishment. "This is incredible!" she gasped. "It seems too good to be true!"

Denny nodded and smiled. "I thought this would be welcome news," he replied. "I was not aware of the fact that your husband had passed away, but it looks as if his planning and foresight will provide for your future."

He cleared his throat. "The only thing we need from you are the filing fees to record your ownership of mineral rights as the lease is processed. Your first royalty check should arrive within sixty days."

"How much are the filing fees?" the woman asked, hesitantly.

Denny consulted a notebook. "Forty-two fifty, ma'am," he told her.

"That's not much," the woman responded. "Will you take a check?"

Denny looked apologetic. "I'm sorry, Mrs. Adams," he explained, "but it's against company policy. Our company has had a real problem with bad checks recently. It's sad, but we're living in a society of thieves. We have to have cash, a money order or a certified check."

"Can you come back this afternoon?"

Denny shook his head. "I'm sorry, but I have several other appointments today, and this is my last day in this area until next month. Perhaps cash would be best. I'll give you a receipt, of course."

Mrs. Adams shrugged, then turned into the house, with the document still in her hands. "Wait a moment. I'll find it somehow."

Half an hour later Denny stopped at another farmhouse to ask directions to the residence of the next customer. He turned to Prince as he climbed back into the van. "It's a good racket, pooch," he said. "Just the mention of unexpected royalties, and these old biddies pay the filing fees without even bothering to check my story. I guess greed overcomes their cautious nature."

He laughed. "Actually, I guess you could say that we're doing these old ladies a favor. Just think of the comfort they receive from thinking they now have a regular income and believing that their husbands had arranged it! I make a decent living, and the poor widow is comforted right at the time of her greatest sorrow. It's a good deal all around."

He pulled up in front of a large dwelling at the edge of town. The two-story brick house was surrounded by acres of well-kept green lawns, and the Oriental garden at the side of the house was complete with bonsai trees, goldfish ponds and a sparkling fountain.

Denny opened the van door for Prince. "We'll do

well here, kid," he said. He took a folder from the back of the van, opened it to check the name on the document against the name on his list, then approached the house and rang the doorbell.

A young man opened the door. "It's best that Mrs. Berryman not be disturbed right now," he said in answer to Denny's request. "Perhaps I can help you."

"My business with the lady is of a rather personal nature," Denny informed him. "It would be best if I talked with her in person. I believe that what I have to say will be a real help to her."

Ten minutes later, as Denny and Prince left the house, a fashionably dressed woman stood by the marble pillars on the porch clutching the worthless document inscribed with her name. Tears streamed down her face as she watched the man and his huge dog walk down the shrub-lined driveway.

"Sixty-five dollars!" Denny told Prince as the big dog leaped into the van. "Some places you can get a little more, and Mrs. Berryman is blessing the name of her departed husband, even though he had nothing to do with it!" He laughed as he started the van.

After two more such visits, Denny turned the van onto the highway and began to drive south again. "So that was the town of Stockton," he said. "We did all right there. Not a bad place to visit, but let's put some miles between us and this joint."

Nearly an hour later the highway crossed a tree-lined stream, and Denny abruptly pulled the van to the side of the highway. The vehicle bounced and jolted as he drove into the shade of the willows lining the banks.

Denny opened the van door for Prince, then slid a tackle box and fishing rod from the side door. "If I have a weakness," he told the Labrador, "it's fishing. I just can't pass up a good fishing place, and this little brook looks like a trout stream to me. What say we go find out?" Prince jumped up and licked the man's face.

Denny set the tackle box on the grassy bank, then opened the lid and selected a bright yellow-and-black fly. He tied the lure to the end of a two-pound test line, checked the knot, then expertly whipped the fly out to light gently in the middle of a riffle caused by a submerged rock. Prince watched the man for a moment or two, then went exploring in the bushes.

When Denny called Prince to the van an hour later, he had a total of three trout. "We'll have 'em for supper tonight," he promised the dog. "We'll stop in the next town we come to and find us a motel room, a newspaper and some cornmeal. Fresh trout for supper tonight!" he whistled as he pulled back onto the highway.

That night in the motel room Denny copied five names from the obituary section of the paper. He brought a small machine in from the van and plugged it in. The smell of hot metal filled the little room as the machine heated up. The man chose five certificates from his stock in the van, then carefully imprinted the names from the paper in gold letters on the documents.

When he was finished, he stood back and looked over the certificates lying on the bed. "That's all there is to it!" he told Prince, who was sniffing at the certificates. "Five names from the paper, five new customers! It's simple. I'll have you doing it in no time."

The next afternoon Denny stood on the porch of the fifth "customer," facing a tall, scowling man at the door. "Mr. McDonald left Anna over a year ago," the man told Denny, "so I know he didn't include her in no land deal before he died. I suggest you take your mineral rights and get off this property fast!" He slammed the door.

Denny walked back to the van. "Well, you can't win 'em all!" he told Prince. He crumpled the certificate into a ball and tossed it into the back of the van, then climbed in. "Four out of five ain't bad, though," he said. "Let's hit the highway. There's more customers waiting."

And so it went. Denny O'Brien, con artist, would hit a town, make four or five deals, then put at least an hour's drive between him and the "customers" before he stopped for the night. Any town large enough to have a newspaper was a potential target. The obituary section of the paper gave the man the information he needed to pull off his scheme.

Prince stayed with Denny for almost a week. The man was working his way south, and it was as if the big dog sensed that the clever con artist was taking him toward home at a pace much faster than he could go on his own.

On Saturday evening Prince waited in the van while the man bought supplies at a supermarket. "Tonight we camp out," Denny told the dog as he climbed into the van with a sack of groceries. "Tomorrow's Sunday, and it's our day off. I'm a man of principles, so I never work on Sunday." He laughed. "And besides, the widow ladies might get suspicious if I approach them on Sunday."

That evening the light from the campfire danced and flickered on the side of the van. Chin on his paws, Prince lay watching Denny grill steaks over the fire on a sturdy forked stick. A can of beans, its top removed, rested in the coals at the fire's edge. "Supper will be ready in just a moment, old pooch," the man said.

Prince suddenly perked up, listening intently. A shadowy figure emerged from the darkness on the other side of the fire, and the dog growled a low warning. "Call yore dog off, pal," the tall, unshaven man said to Denny as he strode toward the fire. "He don't seem friendly."

"Pooch, it's okay," Denny said quietly. He turned to face the man, who was wearing a greasy flannel shirt, dirty denim jeans and a well-worn cowboy hat. "What's on your mind?"

The man smiled. "Just gonna ask ya fer a smoke, neighbor," he replied. "I'm fresh out."

"Sorry," Denny told the taller man. "I don't smoke, so I can't help you."

At that moment another figure slipped out of the darkness behind Denny. Prince growled again. Denny whirled around just in time to duck as the second man swung a heavy branch at his head. The con artist straightened up and lashed out at the man with his fist, striking him soundly in the jaw. There was a grunt of pain from the attacker.

The first man was on Denny in an instant. He punched the smaller man twice, then whipped a long knife from his belt. "Don't be asking for trouble, mister!" he snarled. "We want yore cash—all of it!"

Prince sprang for the man with the knife. Growling his rage, the big dog sank his fangs into the man's right forearm. Immediately the man dropped the knife, gripping his wounded arm with his other hand, howling in pain and anger. His partner leaped forward and swung his tree branch club with all his might. The blow caught Prince across the shoulders, knocking him to the ground.

Stunned, the big Labrador tried to struggle to his feet, but the heavy branch crashed down on his head, knocking him down again. The limb struck twice more, and the big dog lay still.

* * *

Prince opened his eyes, then slowly staggered to his feet. The attackers were gone, and the campfire was slowly dying. The big dog found Denny lying facedown beside his van. He nudged the man gently, whining softly, but the man didn't move. Somehow Prince sensed that Denny would never get up again. His friend would never con another widow.

The big dog limped down to the river and drank

deeply. He lay down on the bank, rested for a few moments, then drank again. He walked over and sniffed at Denny's body, then headed back toward the highway. He traveled south at a slow trot.

Chapter 20

DOGFIGHT

The weather was rapidly turning cooler, and the leaves were reluctantly disappearing from the trees. The wind gusted and moaned like a living thing, scattering the brown and golden fallen leaves as it passed. Summer was gone.

Prince was now less than a hundred miles from home. The journey had been hard and the miles long, but the big Labrador was nearing the end.

His pace quickened now, as if he sensed that he was nearing the end of his long journey. He trotted through fields and valleys, through towns and villages, his head held high. He would soon be with the people he loved. At the pace he was now keeping, the big Labrador would be home in two days.

Early in the afternoon on the second day, however, he entered the city of Visalia, less than seventy miles from Bakersfield, home of the Pattersons. As he cautiously toured the town looking for something to eat, his ears caught the sound of other dogs snarling, yelping and snapping. It sounded like a dogfight was in progress, so the big Labrador hurried toward the sound.

Prince entered an alley and spotted the cause of all the commotion. A large gray mongrel and a liver-colored boxer had a small white terrier cornered behind a shed, intent on tearing her apart. The little dog was doing her best to hold her own. Tail to the fence, she met each advance of the bigger dogs with snarls and lunges of her own.

Her defense had been somewhat effective too. The two aggressors had paid a price when they took on the smaller dog. The boxer was limping, his front right foot badly gashed by the fangs of the little terrier. The mongrel had blood pouring down his face from wounds inflicted by the smaller dog. But the little terrier was slowly losing. Her head was bloody, and she was limping. She had nearly lost one paw to the jaws of one of the attackers, and her coat was torn and mangled in several places. She had put up a tremendous fight, but it was obvious that she could not hold out much longer against the savage attacks of the larger dogs.

With an angry growl, Prince entered the one-sided battle. He charged the boxer and by sheer weight and momentum knocked him off his feet. Snarling and snapping fiercely, Prince went for the other dog's throat, but the boxer squirmed free and dashed to safety.

The big Labrador leaped on the mongrel, who had the little dog by the throat and was shaking her like a rat. Growling in fury, Prince charged at the other dog's flank. Blood from the wound dampened the mongrel's fur, but still he held the yelping little dog in a death grip.

Prince got a grip on the mongrel's leg and bit down hard. With a yelp, the other dog finally released the howling dog, but the boxer reentered the fray. He suddenly appeared around the corner of the shed, lunging straight at Prince.

Prince met the charge head on. The two dogs collided with such force that it seemed that their necks should have been broken. Both dogs fought furiously, but the boxer, quickly realizing that he was no match for the massive Prince, ran from the alley, tail between his legs. Prince whirled to face the mongrel, but the other dog had already fled.

The victorious Labrador advanced, tail wagging, to touch noses with the little terrier, who was licking her wounds and softly whimpering. The smaller dog had just a stump of a tail, but she wagged her entire hindquarters in welcome when Prince came near. After a brief greeting, the little terrier went back to licking her wounds.

Prince lay down in the gravel beside the smaller dog and began to lick a gash that the boxer had inflicted on his right front leg. When he stood up, the little white terrier whined, then struggled to her feet. With her badly mangled paw dangling beneath her, she painfully hobbled over and licked the big dog's nose.

When Prince left the alley, the wounded little terrier was right on his heels, traveling as fast as she could on three legs. The bigger dog slowed so that she could keep up. They walked side by side for several blocks, then the terrier had to stop and rest. The bigger dog came back to her as she lay beside the curb and began helping her lick her wounds. After resting a few minutes, the little white dog struggled to her feet and painfully followed after Prince. Several blocks later, the terrier stopped for a rest in the shade of a pyracantha bush and was soon fast asleep. Prince waited close by, standing guard while his new little friend slept.

Hours later, when the Labrador had finally escaped the confines of the city and reached the open expanses of countryside, the badly mauled little creature was still bobbing alongside, doing her best to keep up.

The two dogs began to travel together. Buzzy, the

little white terrier, had been deserted to the streets when her elderly owner had passed away. For several weeks she had been roaming the streets and alleys of town, learning the life of a homeless dog. In Prince, the lonely little dog had finally found a protector and companion.

They stopped that night at the entrance to a gently sloping canyon. A small stream trickled across the rocky canyon floor, and both dogs drank eagerly. Buzzy found a depression in the rocks at the mouth of the canyon, lay down in it, and soon was fast asleep. Prince watched her for awhile, then quietly left to go hunting.

Twenty minutes later the big dog laid a squirrel on the rocks near the sleeping little dog. When Buzzy awoke and struggled to her feet, Prince picked up the kill and dropped it at the smaller dog's feet. The terrier sniffed at it quizzically, but didn't recognize it as food. She walked stiffly down to the brook and drank deeply again, then returned to her resting-place. Prince lay down beside her, the squirrel still untouched.

The next morning dawned cool and cloudy. Prince was eager to be off and traveling, but Buzzy was stiff and sore from her wounds. The bigger dog coaxed and prodded her until she finally struggled to her feet and followed him. But the traveling was slow. The little terrier, badly injured, had to stop repeatedly to rest. A huge gash in the side of her neck began to bleed again, and she was rapidly growing weaker. Finally, after a hard, slow day of traveling, the pair stopped for the night at the edge of a wooded glen.

Buzzy fell asleep at once, and Prince went in search of game. He was successful almost immediately and returned to the little terrier as soon as he had eaten. The smaller dog was still sleeping, and Prince curled up close beside her.

When a light rain began to fall, the two dogs shivered with the chill of the cold night. Buzzy whined and moaned in her sleep, and Prince woke from time to time. He sniffed the night air, moved closer to the sleeping terrier, then drifted back to a fitful sleep.

The first few streaks of light were brightening the eastern sky when Prince awoke. He stood and stretched, then nudged Buzzy with his muzzle, but she did not respond. He trotted down to the bottom of the hill, drank from a puddle of rainwater, then went in search of food. Half an hour later he returned to the glen, unsuccessful and hungry.

Buzzy was still curled beneath the bushes. Prince

barked softly to awaken her, but the small dog did not stir.

Eager to start traveling, he barked again, louder and more insistent, but the little terrier remained still, her nose tucked under her hind leg.

Prince crawled beneath the bushes and nudged her gently, but she was cold and stiff. The brave little terrier had died during the night.

Suddenly realizing his loss, Prince sat at the edge of the glen and howled mournfully. He was alone again.

Chapter 21
POOR TIMING

David Patterson sighed as he finished the chapter of the mystery he was reading. He dog-eared the next page, then closed the book, dropping it on the end table with a plop that made his mother jump. "Good night, Mom and Dad," he called. "I'm heading for bed."

Mr. Patterson nodded, glancing up from the newspaper. "Good idea, Pal," he said. "We've got a long day ahead of us tomorrow. We'll be getting up pretty early."

He looked at Christina, who was playing on the rug with her Lincoln log set. "You too, Tiger," he said. "Head for bed. You don't want to be tired and grouchy when we get to Grandma's house."

David paused at the foot of the stairs. "How long will it take us to drive there, Dad?"

Mr. Patterson shrugged. "Ten or eleven hours," he replied. "It's over six hundred miles. We'll be there about suppertime tomorrow night."

David climbed the stairs, and Mrs. Patterson turned to Christina, who was slowly dumping the Lincoln logs into their bucket. "Hurry a bit,

Sweetheart," she said. "You need to be in bed."

The little girl snapped the lid on the bucket, then looked up at her parents as a thought suddenly occurred to her. "How long will we be at Grandma's?" she asked, a worried look troubling her pretty features.

"We'll be there for three days," her father explained. "We'll travel all day tomorrow and get there tomorrow evening. We'll have Wednesday, Thanksgiving Day and Friday at Grandma's. Then we'll drive back home on Saturday."

"What if Prince comes while we're gone?" the little girl said, worry in her voice. "He won't know where we are!"

Mr. and Mrs. Patterson looked at each other, then back to Christina. "Head for bed, Christina," Dad said finally. "Prince won't come while we're gone."

"But, Daddy, he might!" the girl argued. "He might come and…"

Her father cut her off: "Christina, head for bed, and quit worrying about Prince! He won't come while we're at Grandma's!"

Pouting, Christina turned and headed up the stairs. She undressed, climbed into bed and fell asleep quickly. That night she dreamed of Prince.

* * *

Unknown to the Pattersons, their huge dog was now less than forty miles from home. He had kept a watchful vigil beside the body of the ill-fated Buzzy for most of the day. As the sun was setting, he had finally left her side and had resumed his southward journey. He would travel all night.

* * *

Mr. Patterson smiled as he glanced at his watch. Ten minutes till eight. The camper was loaded, and in five minutes they would be on the highway. If all went well, they would reach Daisy's before seven o'clock.

David opened the back door of the camper and thrust his BB gun inside. "Dad," he asked, "where will we sleep when we get to Grandma's?"

"We'll sleep in the camper, Son," his father answered, checking his watch again. "We'll just park in Grandma's backyard, between the house and that little barn of hers."

Mrs. Patterson appeared on the porch. "Kenneth," she called, "we have a problem. Christina insists that she wants to leave dog food out for Prince, just in case he comes home while we are gone."

The tall man groaned. "Dog food?" he echoed. "We don't even have any!"

His wife nodded. "That's what I thought. But she has some hidden in the garage, squirreled away out of that bag we gave to the Andersons when we lost Prince."

Mr. Patterson scowled and looked again at his watch. "Tell her to get in the truck—now! We're hitting the road."

Sobbing, Christina squeezed in between her mother and David. Mr. Patterson locked the front door of the house, then hobbled to the truck. He poked his crutches into the space behind the seat, then swung his body in and closed the door. The motor purred to life, and the truck pulled out into the street.

"We'll get gas," Mr. Patterson said, "then hit the highway. Granny O'Dell, here we come, ready or not!" He grinned, trying to be cheerful, but Christina let out a mournful sob.

* * *

Less than a mile away, a huge, tired Labrador trotted wearily across the highway. A horn blared and tires squealed as a motorist braked frantically, the skidding car missing the dog by mere inches. Prince hadn't even seen the car. His attention was elsewhere. He was almost home. He would soon be with the people he loved.

* * *

Mr. Patterson glanced at his daughter as he pulled out of the service station. Seeing tears rolling down her chubby cheeks, he looked over at his wife and shrugged helplessly, giving her one of those "What do you think?" looks. She nodded, wordlessly. With a sigh, he turned the camper around and headed back for the house.

David sat up straight. "Hey! What are we doing?"

Mr. Patterson laid a hand on his knee. "Just running back to the house for a minute," he answered. "Christina is afraid that Prince is going to come to the house while we are gone."

David snorted his disgust. "We're gonna be late getting to Grandma's," he said.

Dad pulled the truck into the driveway. "Why don't you two stay here," he suggested to his wife and son. "Christina and I will just be a minute."

He unlocked the garage. Christina scurried in and knelt in front of his workbench, then pulled two small plastic bags from under the bottom shelf. "I've been keeping them here for Prince," she explained, "so he'll have something to eat when he comes home."

Mr. Patterson nodded. "Of course." He hobbled into the kitchen and returned with a large plastic dish, which he handed to his daughter. "Here. Use this."

Christina emptied the bags into the dish, then set it on the front porch. "There," she said, satisfied, "now Prince will have something to eat if he comes while we are at Grandma's."

They climbed back into the camper, and Mr. Patterson carefully backed out into the street. "No more delays," he said as he shifted into gear. "Let's make some miles for Grandma's house!"

* * *

Prince trotted happily around the corner onto Mulberry Street. He was home at last! The long journey was over. The trip had taken him more than a thousand miles across four states, but at last he had made it. He was home! He knew that a joyful welcome awaited him at the Pattersons.

As he broke into an eager lope and hurried down the block, he spotted the familiar camper backing out of the driveway. Barking joyfully, he raced to meet it, but the vehicle rolled forward and began to pick up speed.

Prince raced toward the camper, barking and

whining, but he soon fell behind. The Pattersons were leaving. He had traveled more than a thousand miles to find them; now they were leaving him!

Dejected, he finally slowed to a stop in the middle of the street, staring after the departing vehicle.

Chapter 22

END OF THE ROAD

David and Christina both heard the sound at the same instant. It was a familiar sound, one which Christina had been constantly praying for and which David had long ago despaired of ever hearing again.

"Daddy, it's Prince!" Christina squealed happily. "I heard him!"

Her father turned to her. "Christina, that's enough! This thing with Prince has gone far enough! Not another word about him!"

David leaned forward across his sister and stared into the right-hand rearview mirror. His eyes grew wide. "Dad!" he shouted. "Stop the truck! It *is* Prince! Stop the truck!"

Mr. Patterson turned to him in disgust as he accelerated down the street. "Not you too, David!"

"It is, Dad, it is!" the boy insisted. "It's Prince! Stop the truck! Look in your rearview mirror!"

With a heavy sigh, Mr. Patterson turned and glanced into the mirror. As he did, his mouth actually fell open in amazement. He hit the brakes so hard that his three passengers were thrown against the dashboard.

"I don't believe it!" he said, watching the huge dog in the mirror. "It really is Prince! He's come home!"

He threw the truck into reverse with such force that his family bumped against the dashboard again. "Look, Honey, look!" he cried to his wife. "It's Prince! It really is!" He brought the truck to a stop twenty yards from the big dog, who bounded forward to meet them with barks of joy.

Mr. Patterson scrambled from the cab as soon as the vehicle came to a stop. In his excitement, he completely forgot his crutches, and as a result he sprawled in the street beside the truck. Mrs. Patterson opened her door, but both of the kids had scrambled across her and were out of the truck before she even set a foot on the pavement. Laughing and crying at the same time, David and Christina hugged the wriggling dog again and again. It was a moment of pure joy.

"You came home, Prince!" Christina cried in delight. "Oh, goody! I knew you would!" She looked heavenward.

"Thank You, Jesus!"

David hugged the big Labrador again. "Prince, it's good to have you home! I can't believe you really made it!"

Mr. and Mrs. Patterson came hurrying up just

then. "It really is him!" Mrs. Patterson exclaimed. "It really is!" She knelt in the middle of the street to hug the delighted dog, then turned to her husband and whispered, "How's this for a lesson in faith?"

Mr. Patterson leaned over and grabbed the huge head in both hands, stroking and petting Prince again and again. "Welcome home, boy! Welcome home!" He glanced up the lane, then turned quickly to his family. "We'd better get out of the street," he suggested. "Cars are waiting to get by."

The Patterson vehicle was right in the middle of the street, and four cars were waiting to get by—three in back of the camper and one in front.

Mrs. Patterson climbed into the back of the camper with Prince and the kids, and Mr. Patterson hobbled to the cab, scrambled in, then pulled to the side of the road in front of a parked car so the waiting vehicles could pass. He turned around in a driveway, then quickly drove back down the block and pulled into his own driveway.

The family piled from the camper, then hugged the happy dog all over again. "Oh, look, Kenneth," Mom cried, pointing to the wound on Prince's cheek. "He's been hurt!"

Dad nodded. "Looks like he's been in a fight recently," he observed. "And he looks like he's exhausted. I'll bet he's had a rough trip!"

The tall professor carefully knelt in the driveway, then laid his crutches on the cement. He ran his hands over the dog, then lifted one front paw and examined it, then looked at the other. "I think he needs a good rest," he told his family. "He's had a rough trip, wherever he's been."

He glanced at his wife, then at David and Christina. "I think it would be best if we call Buck and ask him to tell Grandma we're gonna be a day late. We'll still be in time for Thanksgiving dinner, but Prince is in no shape to travel today. A day of rest will do him good."

The family nodded in agreement, but disappointment was evident in their faces. "I'll go call Buck," Mrs. Patterson said quietly. "I'm sure Mom will understand."

Christina's tears of joy fell into the big dog's fur. "I knew you'd come home, Prince! I knew it! I asked God to help you come back, and He did! Oh, goody!"

"Let's take Prince inside," Mr. Patterson suggested, "then I think we need to stop and thank God for answering Christina's prayer." He smiled suddenly. "And then I think I'll give Professor Dave Andrews a call and tell him God does answer prayer."

Chapter 23

THANKSGIVING

Daisy O'Dell sat in her rocker on the porch with Christina curled up in her lap, while Prince lay at her feet. The big Thanksgiving meal was over. Buck O'Dell was in the kitchen helping Kenneth Patterson with the dishes. The rest of the family were scattered across the porch steps, the porch railing and the three ladder-back chairs beside Daisy's rocker.

"I never dreamed that my Hero was really your Prince," the old woman said happily. "When he left here, it nearly tore my heart out. I never expected to see him again."

"Prince had to leave," Christina declared. "Jesus knew that he belonged to us, and He told him to go home."

Her grandmother smiled. "I guess He did, Sweetheart," she agreed.

"Grandma, will you tell us about the night he came to you?" David asked, and the old woman nodded in agreement.

"It was late in the evening," she began, and her little audience leaned forward eagerly. She told of the shock of finding the big dog by the gate, the desperate struggle as she and Doc fought to save his life, and the happiness the big dog's companionship had brought to her life. As she finished, Buck and Kenneth came out on the porch.

"Have Hero—I mean Prince—show his tricks, Grandma," Lisa pleaded.

The old woman laughed. "Get his newspaper," she requested, and the girl hurried into the house.

The family laughed in delight as the huge dog repeatedly fetched the rolled-up newspaper as it was thrown, then dropped it unerringly at the feet of whichever person Daisy named. Even the adults were mystified.

"How does he do it, Mom?" Alice Patterson asked.

But the old woman just shook her head. "That's Hero's...I mean Prince's secret," she responded. "I promised him I wouldn't tell."

But the trick that delighted little Christina was when Grandma pointed her finger "gun" at Prince and fired. The big dog fell to the ground motionless, then came back to life at her command. The little girl soon discovered that Prince would do it for her also, and she had him repeat the trick again and again.

Finally her mother intervened. "I think that's

enough, Sweetheart. Let's give Prince a rest for awhile, shall we?"

The two days at Grandma's passed all too quickly. Saturday morning Daisy O'Dell stood alone on her front porch, waving as the Patterson camper disappeared down the gravel road in a cloud of dust. Dabbing at her eyes with her handkerchief, she turned and walked slowly into the little house.

Mr. Patterson turned the truck onto the highway and accelerated smoothly. He was alone in the cab. The trip for him would be unusually quiet.

Back in the camper, Mrs. Patterson sat at the tiny dinette and tried to read a book. Two happy, noisy kids laughed as they wrestled on the bed with their huge, playful Labrador. The woman looked up from her book, watched the happy trio on the bed for a moment, then sighed in contentment.

"'If ye shall ask any thing in my name, I will do it,'" she quoted softly. It had been a good trip.